"Look at me,"
Ben demanded.

His hand at her chin pulled sharply when she refused. "Stacey, look at me."

Her eyes flared wide, reflecting defiance and arousal, the icy disdain she'd so carefully cultivated forgotten. Their eyes, blue boring into blue, locked and held, exchanging heat and anger, years of resentment and hurt and desperate need. She felt her resistance melting away as the flicker of memory in his eyes became a blue flame, devouring her.

"No," she managed to say—whether to him or to her own suddenly raging libido she didn't know, couldn't tell. "No," she said as he bent his head toward hers. Her voice was weaker this time. Her hands against his chest unclenched to curl sensuously in the damp, clinging black hairs. His heart was beating like a drum, she realized.

"Oh, no." It was a last, almost silent plea, but her lips were parted in a perfect O of invitation.

Candace Schuler is originally from Texas, but until she wrote *Wildcat* she'd never set a romance there. Perhaps that's because her frequent moves and extensive travel have provided her with a whole world of settings to choose from. Even during the writing of *Wildcat* she was relocating to Minnesota. She and her husband bought a house there, which Candace proceeded to remodel—an enterprise that she assures us will eventually appear in one of her books.

Books by Candace Schuler

HARLEQUIN TEMPTATION

28–DESIRE'S CHILD
102–DESIGNING WOMAN
129–FOR THE LOVE OF MIKE
183–HOME FIRES
205–SOUL MATES
250–ALMOST PARADISE
261–SOPHISTICATED LADY

Wildcat

CANDACE SCHULER

Harlequin Books

TORONTO • NEW YORK • LONDON
AMSTERDAM • PARIS • SYDNEY • HAMBURG
STOCKHOLM • ATHENS • TOKYO • MILAN

To my mother,
Dorothy Jeanette Shaffer,
who kept asking,
"But what about your Texas story?"
until I finally got busy
and did something about it.

Thanks, Mom.

Published January 1990

ISBN 0-373-25384-2

1

STACEY RICHARDS was angry. Furiously angry. The emotion surged through her still body like molten lava heaving unseen beneath the hardened crust of the earth. She closed her eyes, letting herself flow with the feeling for just a moment, almost overwhelmed by the unexpectedness of it. It was the first emotion she'd felt toward her grandfather in the past, endless forty-eight hours.

In the past eleven years.

She didn't count the tears shed yesterday in Marta's motherly arms. They hadn't been for her grandfather but for herself. Tears of weariness, mostly, after the long trip by plane and car, tears of relief and, callous as it might seem, tears of simple happiness at being home again.

I'm home, she'd thought, *and there's no one who can ever send me away again.*

And now this!

Her first impulse was to give in to her anger, to whirl furiously and scream out her rage, but her years at an exclusive school for the daughters of the well-to-do stood her in good stead. She remained facing the window, her proud straight back to the rest of the room, gazing with unseeing eyes at the quiet, sun-scorched courtyard outside. Not by the flicker of an eyelash did she betray how her grandfather's last wishes had hurt and shocked her.

"Do continue, Mr. Barnes," she said to the lawyer, who had fallen silent as if waiting for her reaction. A faint

French accent marred what had once been a molasses-thick West Texas drawl. "I'm sure there's more."

She could sense the men in the room looking at each other, wondering silently at her uncharacteristic lack of response. The Stacey of old would have been halfway into a beauty of a tantrum by now. But she wasn't the Stacey of old. Not by a long shot. "Mr. Barnes?" she said coolly, prompting the still-silent man.

Emmett Barnes cleared his throat and resumed reading Henry "Iron" Oakes's last will and testament. But Stacey was no longer listening. Everything it had to say that concerned her and her future had been said. She stood, still facing the window, and watched a large overweight tabby cat wander aimlessly across the courtyard, wondering if it could possibly be the same cat Marta had had eleven years ago.

Eleven years, she thought. *Eleven wasted years.*

They hadn't really been wasted, of course. On the contrary, they'd been worthwhile and productive years. But they slipped away as she stood there, disappearing in the wavering heat outside the window, and she saw herself as she'd been eleven years ago, right here in this very room.

SHE'D BEEN ANGRY then, too. Furiously angry and hurt and rebellious. You're going away to school they told her, leaving no room for argument on that point. But her grandfather, apparently touched by her furious tears, had softened and allowed her to choose where.

"Paris," she'd said defiantly, picking the most foreign, most wicked place her fifteen-year-old mind could imagine. "Paris or nowhere," she'd insisted, hoping he'd say no.

Her grandfather had almost weakened. She could see she'd been getting to him. Paris was so far away from their ranch in West Texas, not only geographically but culturally, as well, and she was so young. She could see her grandfather was wavering, but Ben spoke up then, insisting that she go, and old "Iron" Oakes had finally agreed.

Her grandfather had made her angry, but she was used to his pigheaded stubbornness and could understand it, having inherited so much of it herself. If it had been just him she would probably have cooled down enough to see the logic of his decision. She'd have eventually settled happily into school, coming home each Christmas and summer vacation and then for good when she graduated. It had been Ben's betrayal that hurt so much, hardening her heart against them both.

She'd always loved Ben, it seemed. First with the worshipful adoration of a child for an older brother or favorite uncle, changing imperceptibly over the years into the shy unspoken love of a young girl for a man seven years her senior. Then, the summer that she turned fifteen, she'd blossomed into womanhood so swiftly that the change seemed to have happened overnight. Along with the curves and the luster that came with suddenly finding herself attractive to the opposite sex had come a teasing seductiveness. She'd become a woman—fully grown, she thought—and she'd waited impatiently but confidently for Ben's declaration.

She'd been so sure that he knew how she felt. So sure that he felt the same and had only been waiting for her to grow up a little before declaring his love. And then he'd shattered her confidence, banishing her from his presence and the home she loved in one fell swoop.

"She's growing up wild," he told her grandfather. "Look at her!" He clamped one hand on the back of her neck. "Skintight jeans, a shirt that almost buttons, hair as wild as a range pony's. She looks like a border-town tart!"

"Take your damned hands off me, you damned horse's ass!" Stacey raged, kicking back at him with her booted feet.

His hand closed tighter on her neck and he lifted her so that she was standing on her toes. She reached up and behind her with both hands, grabbing his wrist, swearing at him all the while.

"Let me go, you son of a—"

A button popped on her shirt front, strained past holding by the pressure of her upraised arms. It let go with a ping, momentarily freezing the actions of the three people in the room, and rolled across the polished wood floor, unnaturally loud in the sudden silence. Stacey gasped, her face burning with embarrassment, her hands dropping to pull her shirt together—but not before both men had seen, quite clearly, that she wore no bra beneath the Western-cut shirt.

"You see what I mean?" Ben said fiercely, letting her go.

"You talk like I did that on purpose," Stacey flared defensively. "I didn't. It was your fault, damn you!"

Ben lifted an eyebrow at her grandfather as if to say, See?

"Marta ought to wash your mouth out with soap," Henry Oakes observed mildly. "You talk like one of the hands."

"Marta can't control her anymore," said Ben, tight-lipped. "If she ever could."

"I don't need anyone to control me."

"The hell you don't!" Ben's voice was low and strained. "Unless somebody stops you from throwing yourself at the hands, you're going to end up the bride at a shotgun wedding."

"That's not true!" Stacey raged. "It's not!"

And it wasn't, not really. The only man she'd wanted, then, was him. She'd only flirted with the hands a little, testing herself and her newfound desirability as any young girl would. Why couldn't he see that?

The battle had raged for another week, but when the smoke cleared Stacey found herself packed up like so much unwanted baggage and put on a plane bound for Paris. The boarding school, recommended by the wife of a friend of her grandfather's, was well-known for its ability to make ladies out of the wayward daughters of the well-to-do.

Stacey eventually adjusted to her new environment. She came to enjoy her school and the friends she made there. Under any other circumstances she might have looked upon the whole experience as an exciting adventure. But she could not—*would not*—forgive Ben and, by association, her grandfather for exiling her from the place and the people she loved best.

Stubbornly, she left her grandfather's short and infrequent letters unanswered until he finally ceased to write to her at all. She wrote instead to Marta. Her letters were full of glowing descriptions of Paris and her new friends and exaggerated tales of one exciting adventure after another. She never mentioned how homesick she was and how bored with fashion shows and museums and cooking lessons and how, if she had to spend one more afternoon at one more charming art gallery, she'd scream.

By the time she was ready to leave school the walls had been built so high that she couldn't knock them down by herself. The only acknowledgment of her graduation from home was a large check from her grandfather with instructions to buy herself "something nice," a drugstore card of congratulations signed "with love" from Ben, and a white lace mantilla from Marta.

She wrote Marta a warm note of thanks, draping the mantilla over her headboard where she could see it each day. She deposited the check in her already bulging bank account; her grandfather would know it had been received when he got the quarterly bank statements. The card, after being read over half a dozen times in the unconscious hope of finding some hidden message, she burned.

No one, not even Marta, had mentioned that now that Stacey was supposedly finished she should come home. And Stacey was too proud, or too stubborn, to say that that's exactly what she wanted to do.

Looking back, she could see what a futile gesture it had been and how, when you came right down to it, she was hurting no one but herself. But she was only eighteen at the time, and older, wiser heads should have prevailed, should have ordered her home. She would have gone, gladly. But no one did.

So Stacey took an apartment in the expensive and fashionable seventh district of Paris and lived as any other young Frenchwoman of considerable means would. She partied far into the night and often right into the dawn. She collected art and drove fast, expensive cars and bought more clothes than she needed or could ever wear. She traveled with friends to Cannes for the film festival, to St. Tropez for the sun and to St. Moritz for skiing. And finally, out of sheer boredom, she found herself a job.

It wasn't a very good job, nor did it pay much. But then, Stacey wasn't working for the money, not with the enormous checks that still arrived every quarter. To her surprise, she found that she liked the business world and that she was good at it. Too good, as it turned out, to be challenged for long by the position she held. Very soon, she began looking around her for new fields to conquer. It didn't take long for her to realize that she wasn't qualified for the kind of job she wanted.

Her obvious enthusiasm and cool blond beauty got her in a lot of doors, but knowing how to set a perfect table, how to pick the proper wine, or how to smooth over sticky social situations—all taught at boarding school— were not readily marketable skills.

So Stacey went back to school. Business school. And when she graduated, two years later, she went to work in the secretarial pool of a small but very wealthy international oil company. In only a year and a half, after a brief stop in the accounting department, she found herself in the enviable position of executive assistant to the president.

It was an exciting and challenging job, made more so by the frequent trips to the company's offices in Saudi Arabia, where Stacey's work took her into the oil fields and refineries as well as the executive suite. Her employer, André el-Hamid, a widower of French-Saudi extraction, had homes in both places, as well as offices, and did a great deal of business-related entertaining so that Stacey's excellent social skills, along with her equally excellent business ones, were finally proving useful.

She was happy she told herself stubbornly when the homesickness became too strong. Paris was her home now and that dusty little podunk ranch in West Texas was just a part of someone she used to be. Her friends, her job, her life were in Paris. She'd be bored silly if she ever had to go back.

But it was a lie. And, deep down, she knew it. She'd have gone home like a shot if anyone had even so much as *hinted* that she was wanted back there. But no one had. Not until the telegram that came less than two days ago.

She'd been spending a long weekend, mixing business with pleasure at the country home of her employer when the telegram finally tracked her down.

HENRY HAD FATAL ACCIDENT. BRONC BROKE HIS NECK. YOU ARE NEEDED IMMEDIATELY FOR READING OF WILL. BEN.

There had been no expression of sympathy, nothing to soften the blow. Stunned, she'd left it to André to express the emotions he felt at the callousness of the missive.

"But this is outrageous!" he bellowed, waving the telegram with Gallic intensity. "Who does this Ben think he is to announce such a calamity with so little sensitivity? Annette—" he called a maid to his side "—pack Mademoiselle Richards's bags immediately and have someone bring the car around. Thirty minutes, no more." He waved the maid away, at the same time drawing Stacey with him out of the room, away from the curious stares of his guests. "I am so sorry, *chérie*," he said in a more normal tone of voice, patting her shoulder comfortingly. "This Henry, he was your father?"

"Grandfather," she corrected him in a small emotionless voice. "André, you don't mind too much, do you? My leaving you in the lurch like this?" She made a vague gesture, which encompassed the guests, her job. "I know there's that contract with Monsieur Jordan to be worked out and a thousand other things, but—" she shrugged "—I'll be back as soon as I can."

"Yes, I will mind. Terribly! But that is of no importance now. Your secretary can handle most of it until your return. And Edouard can help out while you are gone. It will do him good." A hard gleam came into his dark eyes. "It is time that playboy son of mine learned from where comes the jam for his bread," he said, but Stacey didn't laugh as she usually did at André's mangling of American slang. "You go and make ready." He patted her shoulder. "I will call the airport."

"The telegram said immediately, so get me on the first available flight, no matter what the connections are like," she said as she moved toward the stairs. *Home*, a voice sang somewhere in her head, lightening her step as she hurried up to the luxuriously appointed guest room that had been assigned to her. *I'm going home.*

NEARLY EIGHTEEN HOURS and two plane changes later she touched down in Lubbock, Texas. There'd been a stopover of several hours at the Dallas/Fort Worth airport and she'd left the plane, overnight case in hand, to find a ladies room and freshen up. It had helped some but not much, and she still felt rumpled and travel stained and more weary than she could ever remember being before. There was no one familiar to meet her at Lubbock International. Just a lanky young cowboy in faded Levi's and a dusty brown Stetson. He introduced himself, saying, "Hank Watkins, ma'am. Boss sent me to pick you up."

They accomplished the three-hour drive to the ranch in nearly complete silence, the young cowboy having little conversation of his own and Stacey being too tired to draw him out. The air conditioning in the old tan pickup proved inadequate to the Texas sun and they drove with the windows open, both of them preferring the fine, gritty dust to the stifling heat of the closed cab. She sat almost motionless during most of the long drive, her head resting tiredly against the seat back, her eyes barely registering the seemingly endless miles of two-lane highway bordered on both sides by equally endless miles of barbed-wire fence and the flat dusty land that stretched as far as the eye could see.

She seemed to know instinctively, though, when the passing landscape became Iron Oakes land. She straightened, her eyes scanning the horizon eagerly for the first glimpse of the high, arched gate that marked the main entrance to the ranch.

"Stop, please," she instructed the young driver quietly when he turned off the highway, bumping over the metal cattle guard, to pass under the white-painted iron gate.

He pulled to a stop and waited as she got out of the truck. She stood silently, gazing around almost reverently, saying her own private hello to the ranch. She inhaled deeply, breathing in the dust and the heat and the faint, unforgettable perfume of the sparse silvery sage. She could even smell the fainter but no less welcome stench of the oil pumps that dotted the distant horizon. As always, they reminded her of some strange species of insect, though far too many of them were motionless when they should have been pumping the black wealth from beneath the barren-looking ground. It told her, all of it, that she was really, finally home.

She lifted one graceful hand to shade her eyes, straining to see the main house at the end of the long road. She could just make out its outline, surrounded by the huge trees that had been transplanted years ago by her grandfather to shade and protect the house and its inhabitants from the relentless sun. She could see, too, the vague outlines and rooftops of the outbuildings—the barn and bunkhouse and various sheds—that were set out behind and slightly to the south of the main house.

The outbuildings seemed to be bigger than she remembered, and there were more of them. A grain elevator and another barn and several tall, spindly, oddly shaped structures revolving lazily in the almost nonexistent breeze that she finally decided must be some sort of experimental windmills. She sighed, feeling somehow betrayed by these changes to her childhood home, and climbed back into the cab of the truck.

As they got closer to the house she saw even more changes. Small ones in reality, but to Stacey each difference felt like a stab at her heart, and she couldn't see them for the improvements that they were. She closed her eyes wearily, not wanting to see any more, but as the truck bumped over a second set of cattle guards, she opened them again. They had arrived.

The young cowboy busied himself with her suitcases, leaving Stacey to make her own way as he carried them in ahead of her. The tiled front hall was exactly as she remembered it, shadowed and cool after the brutal sun outside. It was full of people, too, or so it seemed to Stacey, who was by then so worn and weary that she could hardly see straight. She saw Ben immediately, though, towering head and shoulders over everyone else in the room.

"Hello, Stacey," he said, his eyes speculative as they ran over her from the sleek coil of her hair to the toes of her snakeskin pumps. "You've changed."

"That was the general idea, wasn't it?" she replied coolly, rising instinctively to the challenge in his voice and his assessing blue eyes.

"It was," he agreed easily. "I'm glad to see that all that money wasn't totally wasted."

Uncle Pete—not a real uncle but, rather, her grandfather's old wildcatting partner—claimed her attention, then, pumping her hand in greeting. He pounded her on the back with his other hand, welcoming her home. And then Ramon, the Iron Oakes gardener and handy man—grown so old now!—made a short welcoming speech, his eyes riveted firmly on the floor as he spoke. Everyone else was new to her. Uncle Pete was just beginning general introductions when Stacey spotted Marta coming toward her like a longhorn cow who had just sighted a lost calf.

"Shame on you," she chided everyone, gathering Stacey to her as if she were no more than ten years old. "Can't you see that she is tired? Worn to the bone! Go, all of you." She leveled a pudgy brown finger at Ben. "You, also, Benito. Go!" She waved them all away and steered Stacey up the wide staircase to the bedrooms on the second floor.

"Come with me, *niña*," Marta said, using the familiar Mexican endearment that Stacey hadn't heard in eleven years. She hustled her charge down the hall. "You are tired, no? Come. You will undress and nap and then, when you have rested, you will eat."

"But lunch," Stacey protested halfheartedly. "I could smell the enchiladas when I came in."

"There will be plenty more when you wake up, *niña*," Marta said, opening a suitcase. She handed Stacey an ivory silk nightgown and pushed her toward the bathroom. "Go wash," she commanded, as if Stacey were a recalcitrant child.

Stacey took the gown and did as she was told, emerging a scant ten minutes later feeling vastly better for the quick wash.

"*Muy bonito*," complimented Marta, fingering the silky material of her nightgown. "You have grown up very pretty. Benito, he will like that, *sì*? Come," she commanded before Stacey could say that she didn't particularly care whether Ben liked the way she'd grown up or not. "Sit here—" she motioned toward the bed "—and brush the tangles from your hair before you sleep. You have had a long trip, no?" she went on, not waiting for, or expecting, an answer as she bustled from the open suitcase to the closet.

Stacey smiled and did as she was told. Marta hadn't changed one iota, bless her; she still treated Stacey like a beloved, if slightly backward, child. "I can do that later, Marta," she said, flicking the brush through her hair.

"Ah, pah!" Marta replied exactly as Stacey had known she would. "It is no trouble. I do it now," she said, citing a familiar refrain, "and it is done. *Sì*?"

"*Sì*," Stacey replied, shaking her hair back as she laid the brush on the nightstand.

Marta's busy hands paused in their task. "So fair still," she mused, "just like when you were a little girl." She reached out, touching Stacey's hair lightly. "You have been away too long, I think. It is good to have you home, *niña*."

"It's good to be home, Marta," Stacey said simply and then, suddenly, without warning, she burst into tears.

"There, there." Marta gathered Stacey comfortingly to her ample bosom. "There my sweet *niña*," she soothed, stroking the shining blond head. "It is all right now. You're home," she chanted, rocking gently until the sobbing quieted and then, finally, ceased. "There! You feel much better now, *sì?*" she said, taking a handkerchief from the bodice of her dress to tenderly wipe the upturned face.

Stacey nodded. "I'm sorry, Marta," she said, taking the handkerchief to finish the job herself. "I don't know what came over me."

"Pah!" Marta made a sound of dismissal, waving aside any explanations or apologies. "You are exhausted," she said. "Come. Into bed."

Smiling, Stacey did as she was told, snuggling gratefully into the cool, crisp white sheets that Marta held open for her. Her eyes drooped heavily. *Heaven*, she thought. *I'm home and it's sheer heaven.*

"Sleep as long as you need to," Marta instructed as she closed the long louvered doors leading to the upper veranda. "When you wake there will be enchiladas and guacamole, *sì?*"

"And Mexican coffee?" came the sleepy question.

"*Sì*, and Mexican coffee," Marta said softly, closing the door behind her as she backed out of the bedroom.

Exhausted, Stacey slept for hours, through lunch and dinner both, waking to full daylight and the furtive sounds of Marta unpacking her suitcase.

"I'm awake, Marta," she said from the bed. "There's no need to be so quiet on my account."

"You have no other black dresses, *niña?*" Marta asked, holding up two delectable Parisian creations obviously meant for evening wear. One was a short, slinky bias-cut satin, the other was a long-sleeved, floor-length sheath with a slit up one side. "Where is your black suit for the funeral?"

Stacey pushed her single cover off and sat up, reaching for the ivory silk robe at the foot of the bed. "There is no black suit. I'll be wearing the dark green dress with the jacket."

"Green! You cannot wear green to your grandfather's funeral. It is not respectful!"

"It's perfectly respectful, Marta," she said firmly, and then added at the housekeeper's reproachful look. "The dress is forest green, after all. You can hardly get any darker than that."

Marta's expression didn't change.

Stacey tightened the belt on her robe and looked away, refusing to feel like a guilty child. "It's not as if I were planning to wear red."

"But you should wear black," insisted Marta, who was herself draped in that color from the lace mantilla that covered her hair to the sturdy, low-heeled shoes on her feet. The worn gold crucifix that Stacey had never seen her without hung on a slender gold chain around her neck. A rosary made of gold filigree and ebony beads was tucked into her belt. "You are his granddaughter."

"His granddaughter that he never saw once in eleven years."

"That was not all his fault, I think."

"No, it wasn't," admitted Stacey, thinking of Ben rather than herself. "But it changes nothing." She paused in gathering together her toilette articles. "I won't be a hypocrite and pretend an emotion I don't feel. Please try to understand, Marta. I can't."

"He missed you terribly," Marta tried one more time.

"Did he?" Stacey shrugged, unmoved. "I find that a bit hard to believe." If he'd missed her, why hadn't he come for her? Why hadn't he, even once, asked her to come home? She paused in the bathroom doorway. "I don't have anything else to wear, anyway, Marta," she said. "Unless you think the beige suit would be better?"

When she finished in the bathroom, Marta was gone. The unpacking had been completed and the bed made. The dark green dress and its matching jacket lay across the ruffled pink bedspread in silent reproach, the white lace mantilla spread out next to it.

Stubbornly refusing to feel guilty, Stacey dressed and did her makeup with a swiftness borne of long practice. She brushed her fine, golden-blond hair away from her face, plaiting it into a sleek French braid, finishing it with a small, flat, grosgrain bow.

The forest green dress was a figure-skimming, linen-look sheath cut with a master hand to subtly hint at the lithesome female form beneath the material. It had a demure boat neck and was sleeveless but the matching jacket made up for that lack, its long sleeves and tailored, boxy styling making her look almost prim.

Defiantly, Stacey added a triple strand of large, milky pearls around her neck, pearl studs in her ears and a discreet spray of expensive perfume before finally draping the lacy mantilla over her head. Then she stepped back and surveyed herself in the large oval mirror over the old-fashioned dresser. *No range pony wildness now*, she thought with satisfaction.

The woman reflected in the mirror looked appropriately subdued, but very chic. She could have been attending the funeral of a business acquaintance. No stranger, seeing Stacey, would suspect that the man being buried today was her grandfather, the man who had raised her from infancy after her parents had been killed.

It struck her suddenly that she hadn't yet seen the body, didn't know what arrangements had been made, didn't know anything at all, really, aside from what had been in Ben's telegram. But it was no use thinking about it now, she told herself. There was nothing she could do about anything at this point, anyway. And Ben had undoubtedly taken care of everything.

BEN DELIVERED THE EULOGY at the graveside, keeping it short and simple, stating the barest statistics of Henry "Iron" Oakes's long and eventful life.

"He died as he would have wanted to, had he been able to choose," Ben said, his deep voice husky with pain. "Quickly, and in the best of cowboy traditions, with his boots on. We must be glad for his sake that it happened that way, no matter how big—" his voice faltered slightly and he paused, visibly gathering himself together "—how big a hole his passing has left in all our lives. We'll miss him." He bent and touched the coffin lightly, almost caressingly. "Goodbye, Henry," he whispered, his blue eyes bright with unshed tears. "God go with you."

Stacey looked away then, feeling as if she were intruding on an intensely private conversation. Seeking something, anything else to focus her attention on, her eyes skimmed over the other mourners gathered around the gravesite.

It was obvious that her grandfather had been well loved and respected, and not only by Ben. The little family cemetery was full to overflowing with ranch hands, friends and neighbors. There were a surprising number of grizzled old men who'd flown in from the nearby oil centers of Houston and Tulsa, as well as from as far away as Anchorage and Mexico City and the oil-rich North Sea off Great Britain's shores. They were old wildcatters like her grandfather and Uncle Pete; some had struck it rich, as "Iron" Oakes had, some had since lost everything in the latest oil bust, and some had never made it at all. But all of them held their hats in their hands in a gesture of respect for a fallen friend.

Marta wept openly, standing there beside Stacey, as did several of the other women. Even Uncle Pete, on her other side, hid suspiciously bright eyes. But Stacey didn't cry. She couldn't. And, standing there, composed and dry-eyed, she could feel the disapproval of those around her. *Unnatural girl,* their eyes said. Stacey stiffened her already straight back and returned the condemning stares with icy dignity. And then the preacher said "Amen" and everyone began filing away from the grave. Ben took her arm, leading her toward a waiting car, and she forgot the disapproving mourners between one breath and the next.

"Emmett Barnes will meet us back at the house," Ben said, settling his big frame behind the wheel of the two-year-old dark blue Lincoln. "He wants to go over Henry's will without any delay."

Stacey reached into her bag for a badly needed cigarette and lit it, completely forgetting that she was trying to quit. "Is all this unseemly haste necessary?"

"Emmett seems to think so. Something in the will's put a burr under his saddle and he wants to get rid of it, pronto." He paused, his glance flickering over her. "It's probably not going to be—"

She stopped him with a toss of her head. The mantilla fell down around her shoulders at the movement. "I'd rather hear it from Mr. Barnes."

Ben shrugged, the fine black cloth of his jacket straining across his wide shoulders. "Suit yourself," he said, and headed the car down the graveled road to the main house.

Stacey sat stiffly, separated from him by two feet of light gray upholstery, and studied him from under her lashes. He'd changed very little in the past eleven years, except to get even bigger and tougher looking, if that were possible, filling out the promise of the broad shoulders that he'd had even as a rangy, wiry teenager.

He'd been fourteen to her six when he first showed up on the ranch, looking for sanctuary with his Aunt Marta after the death of his mother. Over the years, Stacey had learned that his father had been an alcoholic, cold and unfeeling toward his only son when he was sober, abusive when he was drunk. His mother's death had freed him to leave.

Henry had taken an immediate liking to the young Ben, going so far as to invite him to live in the main house like a member of the family. Marta had joyously welcomed him for his own sake, as well as that of her deceased sister, making it part of her life's mission to add weight to his rangy frame. And six-year-old Stacey had unconditionally adored him.

Theirs had been a special relationship then, with Ben filling the role of big brother and protector, Stacey the indulged and adoring kid sister. Two years later, Ben's father died and Henry formally adopted him. Stacey was ecstatic; now Ben was a *real* relative, she'd thought gleefully.

It was then that the rumors started. Ben was the old man's bastard kid, some said behind his back, though no one, not even Ben, knew for sure and none dared ask. Ben had wanted the rumors to be true—even at eight, she'd somehow known that without being told. He'd wanted it fiercely, with all the longing of a boy who'd never known a father's love or basked in the pride that a man was supposed to feel for his only son. Having Henry as his real father would have explained a lot, giving him a reason for the way he'd been treated by the man he'd called father for the first sixteen years of his life.

Stacey had been too young, at first, to understand all the ramifications of the whispered snatches of overhead conversation, despite the fact that she intuitively understood Ben's reaction to them. Years later, when she did understand, she fiercely denied it because if Ben was her grandfather's natural son, it meant he was really her uncle. And she knew you weren't supposed to feel about your uncle the way she was, by then, beginning to feel about Ben.

She studied him now, her eyes not blinded by childish adoration or adolescent infatuation, looking for a resemblance to her grandfather and finding none. Henry Oakes had been fair-haired, as she was, and a smaller man physically than the dark-haired, swarthy-skinned giant who sat beside her now. The only thing you could tell for sure about Ben by looking at him was that he was a Texas rancher.

Even in the somber funeral black his appearance screamed cowboy, she thought. Maybe it was the Western cut of his suit. Or his tan, burned so deep that she doubted he would ever lose it. Or the way his eyes crinkled up at the corners as if he were perpetually squinting into the blazing Texas sun. Or his big, work-callused hands, so strong and capable looking as they rested on the steering wheel. Or—

Her mind veered off suddenly, self-protectively, focusing on the black Stetson on the seat between them, tossed there when he got into the car. *Cowboy*, she thought again, scornfully, trying to imagine a brace of six guns strapped to his long muscular thigh. But he really didn't need them to complete the picture. He had a tough, virile, uncompromising look about him that clearly said he was a man to be reckoned with. A man whom, sooner or later, *she* was going to have to reckon with.

2

"MIZ RICHARDS?" It was the lawyer's voice, calling her back to the present. "Miz Richards?"

Stacey turned from the window to face the three men standing behind her in her grandfather's den, waiting for her reaction to his outrageous will.

The lawyer, Emmett Barnes, stood behind Henry's desk, clearly wishing that he were anywhere but where he was. His hand came up and nervously plucked his shirt collar as if feeling the heat, though the room was cool despite the midsummer sun. His eyes slid away from her steady gaze.

Uncle Pete smiled at her from his place in front of the empty fireplace, a little sheepish, obviously a little worried about what her reaction would be, before returning to his contemplation of the hearth stones.

Only Ben dared to look her squarely in the eyes.

How long his lashes are, she thought irrelevantly, ridiculously long for a man, and as dark as his hair, framing eyes of a startling clear blue. *Almost as blue as mine*, came the unbidden thought, and she wondered again about his parentage. He lounged, apparently completely at his ease, in one of the two big leather chairs facing the desk. His long, hard-muscled legs were stretched out in front of him, the booted feet crossed at the ankles, a well-iced glass of bourbon in one hand. He took a long slow sip, watching her.

"It can be broken, I suppose?" Her words were for the lawyer, but her eyes questioned Ben.

"No, I'm afraid it can't," Emmett Barnes said. "It's ironclad."

"No will is ironclad," Stacey retorted.

"This one is," Ben put in before the lawyer could answer.

"I'm truly sorry, Miz Richards, but I'm afraid Ben's right." Emmett paused, clearing his throat, and then went on uncertainly. "I tried to tell Henry that it was a crazy thing to do, putting it in his will like that. He should have told you his intentions himself. Prepared you."

"Prepared me? As if anything could." Her voice was brittle, and she forced herself to take a deep, calming breath before turning from Ben's measuring gaze to face the lawyer. "I'm sure you did your best, Mr. Barnes— Emmett," she corrected herself. "No one knows better than I what a hard man my grandfather was."

"He was only tryin' to protect you," offered Uncle Pete.

Stacey turned icy blue eyes on him. "From what?"

Pete shrugged and looked down at the toe of his boot.

"He was trying to protect the ranch and his oil companies," she said flatly. "And Ben."

"Now, Stacey, girl," Pete cajoled, trying again. "Be reasonable."

"Was Henry reasonable?" she challenged, her blue eyes glacial as she reached for her sleek leather bag where it lay on a corner of the desk. She rummaged for her cigarette case. "Is this will reasonable?"

"The way he looked at it, he was. It is," Pete said.

"And what about the way I look at it?" She flipped open a gold cigarette case and extracted a long, slender cigarette, lighting it before anyone could move to do it for her. She tossed her head back, inhaling deeply. *Thank heavens for nicotine*, she thought, feeling calm spread through her as the soothing smoke filled her lungs. "Is this will reasonable for me? Or fair?"

She strode angrily to the window and back, her long legs moving gracefully from the hip, pulling the dark green dress tight against the curve of her back with each step. "Did *he once* think about me or how I would feel when this—" her hand arched through the air "—this medieval document was read?"

"Oh, surely not medieval." Ben spoke lazily from the depths of the leather chair.

Stacey whirled, crushing out the just-lit cigarette in an ashtray on the desk as she passed it, and came to stand in front of his chair at the point where his long legs ended.

"Besides," he said, before she could speak, "I can't rightly see what you're squawking about. You'll still be getting your checks regularly." He paused for a moment to emphasize his next words. "If that's what you decide you want."

"You knew," she accused him bitterly. "You knew and you approved, didn't you?"

"No. I didn't know," he said calmly, raising his glass to his lips. He surveyed her over the rim, his eyes traveling slowly from her flushed, angry face to touch lingeringly on her full breasts, rising and falling visibly with her agitation, down to her narrow waist and softly rounded hips, to the long, slender length of her legs, and then back up again.

She'd changed, as he'd said yesterday in the front hall, but not enough to matter. More mature, sleeker, a great deal more polished, maybe, but she was still the most exciting female in the state of Texas. Especially when she was on the verge of a temper tantrum. "But now that I've had a chance to look you over, it doesn't seem like a half-bad idea," he said, just to see if he could push her over the edge. "You grew up real—" a slow, deliberately lascivious smile curved his lips "—nice."

Stacey heard the collective gasp behind her and ignored it, as she tried to ignore her own heightened color. Her reaction wasn't one of outraged modesty, however, or shock that Ben would say such a thing—she told herself she expected no better of him—it was one of overwhelming anger.

She could feel it boiling up in her again, threatening to break the bounds of her hard-won self-control. Her hands clenched by her sides as she imagined hitting him. Or throwing something at his head. With a superb effort of will she forced the feeling down and unclenched her hands as her mouth curved into the semblance of a smile.

"I've had a chance to look you over, too." Her eyes ran disparagingly over the length of him where he lounged in the leather chair. Her smile turned overly sweet and catlike. "Unfortunately, my taste doesn't run to overbearing, ill-mannered, redneck cowpunchers," she said disdainfully. She turned from him, going to sit on a corner of her grandfather's desk.

Her action caused her to miss the admiring gleam that flickered in his eyes for a moment. Stacey had always given as good as she got; he was glad to see that she still did, despite the ice-maiden facade. "You could sell out," he taunted, wondering how far he could push her before the ice would crack clean through.

"And leave you in sole possession of *my* home?" She glared at him through narrowed eyes. "Not a chance. This is my home. My ranch. I've waited nearly eleven years to come back to Iron Oakes, and I'm staying," she said, surprising everyone, including herself. She hadn't intended to stay when she left Paris. She'd told André that she'd be back. "I'm staying," she repeated, realizing that she meant it. "Even if I have to marry a snake like you to do it."

"Now, Miz Richards," Emmett said, claiming her attention as he tried to smooth things over. "There's no need for this unseemly haste."

Her glance flickered unwillingly to Ben for a moment, catching the brief flash of ironic humor. Those had been her exact words to him in the car.

"You have six months to make up your mind, you know," the lawyer went on.

"Six months." She waved her hand in a gesture of dismissal. "And what good does that do me? According to Henry's will, I'd still have to marry Ben at the end of it."

"You might decide to sell your half," Pete began hesitantly and then stopped, wary of the cold light in her eyes as she turned to him.

"No." Stacey's voice was flat and strangely unemotional. "This ranch is half mine and I intend to keep it. And no one—" her icy glance speared Ben for a moment and the glacial lights turned to blue flames "—no one," she repeated, "is ever going to run me off again. No matter what I have to do."

"Yes, of course, but, Miz Richards—"

"You might as well call me Stacey," she said, interrupting the lawyer. "This matter is a little too intimate for us to stand on ceremony, don't you think?" She drew her purse toward her again as she spoke and flipped open the gold cigarette case. This time she held the cigarette to her lips and waited expectantly. It was Emmett who hurriedly drew a lighter from his vest pocket to light it for her.

Stacey nodded her thanks and rose from the edge of the desk, moving with cool, feline grace to sit in the leather chair opposite Ben. The little ritual of the cigarette had given her the time she needed to collect herself. She was in control again.

"I'll have a brandy now, please, Uncle Pete," she said with a slight smile. "Courvoisier, if you have it." She crossed her long, nylon-clad legs and leaned back, deceptively casual. "What about divorce?" she asked Emmett.

"Divorce? Hell's bells, girl, you ain't even married yet," said Pete, handing her the drink in a heavy, straight-sided highball glass.

"I think what the lady means is can she get a quickie Mexico marriage and divorce—"

"Preferably on the same day," Stacey interjected.

"—and still keep half the ranch," Ben finished, ignoring her interruption. "The answer is no."

She looked at Emmett. "Is that right?"

"I'm afraid so, Miz Rich—ah, Stacey. Your grandfather was very specific about that part of the will. If you marry Ben and then later get a divorce, your half of Iron Oakes Ranch reverts to him. Unless there are, ah, children, of course," he said, a red tinge creeping up from under his collar. "In that case, Ben would hold the land in trust until they came of age."

"Even if he beats me?"

"Uh, beg pardon?" Emmett stammered. "Beats you?"

"If I divorce him for cause," she explained, watching Ben for a reaction. She had yet to goad him out of his calm, and he'd pushed her too close to the edge twice already. "You know," she elaborated, "physical brutality, adultery, that sort of thing. Would he still get the ranch?"

"You got no call to go sayin' a thing like that, girl!" Pete exploded, shocked down to his hand-tooled boots. "Ben would never hit no woman." The disapproving look he gave her was darkly significant. "Even if she deserved it."

Stacey barely glanced at him. "Would he?" she persisted, her eyes on Emmett.

"No," he said. "At least, I don't think so," he amended. "Henry made no special provisions as to the cause of divorce."

"I see. So any way you look at it, I lose."

"Not at all," Emmett hastened to reassure her. "This provision of Henry's will applies only to the ranch. Your ownership in other Oakes Enterprises' holdings has nothing to do with whether or not you marry Ben. In fact, you own several oil leases outright—"

"Well, hallelujah," Stacey said dryly, referring to the currently depressed state of Texas oil prices.

"Don't you be scoffing, girl," Pete scolded her. "Things'll turn around soon enough. They always do."

"Yes, that's right," Emmett agreed. "They always do if you can hold on long enough—and there's no question that you can. Henry saw to it that you own some other subsidiary companies of Oakes Enterprises that have nothing to do with oil. It's all right here, if you'd care to read it." He gestured toward the will where it lay on the desk. "If you decide that you can't, ah, comply with this one provision of the will, well, Ben is instructed to pay you a fair market value for half the ranch. Over a reasonable period of time, of course," he added. "But you'd lose nothing financially. In fact, Miz—ah, Stacey, you're a very wealthy young woman. Very wealthy, indeed. With proper management, you'll never want for anything."

"I wouldn't have the ranch."

"No, you wouldn't. But if you'll forgive my saying so, does that matter so much? You haven't lived here since you were fifteen, or so I've been given to understand."

"I was away at school." She blew a cloud of smoke into the air and looked at them through it, silently daring any one of them to refute her words.

"Yes, at first, but more recently by choice," Emmett ventured.

"Not by *my* choice."

"Whose choice, then?" Ben challenged. His voice had a hard, angry edge to it. Who the hell else's choice had it been, if not hers?

"You can ask me that?" Stacey fought the urge to jump up and confront him. "*You?*" she said, her voice like ice. "The low-down snake who convinced my grandfather to send me away in the first place!"

"It was for your own good. And like Emmett said, you weren't at school the whole time, or even most of it. You could have come home anytime you wanted."

Stacey came ramrod straight in her chair. "Anytime I wanted! After the way I was sent away? After no word, not even a lousy postcard?" she said furiously, forgetting the letters that had arrived in the beginning. "Nothing but those damn checks?"

"Whose fault was that?"

"I was fifteen years old!" she defended herself. "A child in a foreign country and away from home for the first time in my life. And you're saying that I should have been the wise one and made the first move?"

"He was a proud man."

"And that excuses him, I suppose?"

"Now, Stacey, girl," Pete soothed uneasily. "Henry was only tryin' to protect you."

"You said that before." She rose with a jerky motion, her cool, calm exterior once again shattered, and moved to stand at the window with her back to the room. "But protect me from what?" she asked after a minute, turning around. "Answer me that, if you can, Uncle Pete. Protect me from what?"

"Well, from—" he shrugged uneasily "—from havin' to come back here, permanentlike, if you didn't want to," he said finally. "You been gone a long time, girl. You might of found yourself a man you didn't want to up and leave."

Stacey's low laugh was bitter. "So he made the provision that I'd have to marry Ben?" she said scornfully. She made a small, disbelieving gesture with her hand that stopped him from thinking up further inane excuses for his old friend. "Henry wrote this will to protect the ranch, to protect Ben, and to punish me," she said, slapping the offending piece of paper with the flat of her hand. Ashes from her cigarette drifted over the desk. "What I can't understand is why he didn't just leave it to Ben outright and save all this argument."

"He knew you'd fight that," Ben said, wondering why the hell Henry hadn't realized that she'd fight this, too. And harder than she would have fought it the other way. He rose from his chair in one fluid motion, graceful for so big a man, and set his empty bourbon glass on the bar.

"But fight this and you stand a good chance of losing it all," he said. "Most Texas juries wouldn't look kindly on a woman who hadn't seen her grandfather—*her only blood relative*," he emphasized, moving toward her as he spoke, "for almost eleven years, fighting like a greedy little bitch to get more. They'd most likely think that you'd got enough already. More than enough, all things considered."

He stopped directly in front of her, deliberately crowding her against the desk. "I think everyone's got a clear idea of how things stand," he said, his eyes touching each of them in turn before coming to rest on Stacey's upturned face.

She stared back at him, her wide blue eyes no longer cool and scornful, but full of the same spit and hellfire as they'd been when she'd gotten angry as a girl. Her finely chiseled jaw was set in the stubborn line he remembered far too well for his own good. Her lush mouth was firmed in anger.

He studied her for a brief moment, the space of a heartbeat only, remembering other times that she had stood just so, staring up at him with daggers in her blue eyes. He'd felt then much as he felt now: frustrated, angry, confused, lustful, not knowing whether he wanted to shake her until her teeth rattled or haul her into his arms and kiss away her bad temper. He hovered for a moment between the two possibilities.

And then Stacey lifted her hand, bringing the half-smoked cigarette to her lips.

Ben frowned and his big hand came up, quick as a cat, swallowing her wrist in his grasp. Before she could twist away he reached up with his other hand and took the cigarette from her. He reached around her to the over-size crystal ashtray on the desk, and crushed it out, ignoring her gasp of protest.

"Nasty habit," he said softly, enjoying the feel of her soft skin beneath his fingers. Had she been this soft eleven years ago? "Not at all ladylike."

Stacey nearly hissed, her anger finally boiling over at his careless assumption of authority. Her fingers curled, the long, beautifully manicured, salmon-pink nails pressing into the back of his hand. He tightened his grip warningly, and then almost painfully, but she persisted, digging her nails into his flesh until they threatened to draw blood.

"You have six months," he said finally, his voice still soft but dangerously so. His eyes were hot as they blazed down into hers. Hot with anger and desire and the wild thrill of standing toe-to-toe with her again.

Stacey returned his glare steadily, giving as good as she got, willing herself to give no outward sign that he'd cowed her. Or aroused her.

Their gazes held for a few seconds more, her nails still pressed into the back of his hand, his fingers still wrapped around her wrist. The two other occupants of the room were silent and still, waiting for the explosion. Seconds ticked by like minutes, neither of them moving, neither of them backing down.

"Hell," Ben swore in disgust and dropped her wrist. He brought his injured hand to his mouth, sucking lightly at the marks that she'd made with her nails. "Marta will have lunch on the table by now and we've wasted enough time already on all this palaverin'," he said, turning toward the door. "I've got work to do yet today."

LUNCH HAD a rather solemn air. Obviously intended by Marta to be both a welcome home to Stacey and a farewell to Henry Oakes, it hovered somewhere in between, neither completely festive nor truly sorrowful.

The table was covered with a fine lace tablecloth and set with delicate crystal glasses and fine English bone china. The silver was Gorham sterling. Stacey stared at it for a moment, surprised. The dining room of her memory had been an uncomfortable and seldom-used room; she remembered eating in the kitchen most of the time, off sturdy crockery.

The table's elegance couldn't be Marta's doing, she knew, because as lovingly as she would care for it, Marta wouldn't know the difference between the finest Waterford crystal and an imitation from the local K Mart. Nor would she care. And neither would Henry or Uncle Pete. They'd been roughneck wildcatters in the early years when they'd first formed their partnership, and despite their success, neither of them had ever given a plugged nickle about the so-called finer things in life.

Which, by the process of elimination, left Ben. But Ben was as much a hick cowboy as Henry had been and Pete still was. Wasn't he?

Something of her bafflement must have shown in her face, for she looked up from her brief contemplation of the beautifully set table to find Ben eyeing her sardonically, as if he knew full well what she was thinking.

We're not all quite the rough country hicks that you'd like us to be, his look said clearly.

Stacey turned her head quickly away from him, forcing herself to smile up at Marta instead. "Oh, how wonderful! Enchiladas," she said as the housekeeper proudly placed a steaming plate on the table in front of her.

If the table was set like something out of *House Beautiful*, the food was pure Tex-Mex, a delicious blending of the Texas and Mexican cuisines. Besides the enchiladas made with homemade corn tortillas, there were soft refried beans without which no Mexican meal was complete, spicy Spanish rice with colorful bits of peppers and pimentos, deep-fried turnovers, filled with savory Gulf shrimp, and Marta's special guacamole. Which was hotter than Hades, Stacey remembered belatedly, reaching for her iced tea, but delicious nonetheless.

"Enough," she said at last when Marta offered second helpings of the traditional caramel-topped flan she was serving for dessert. "It's wonderful, all of it, but I've had enough."

"You are too skinny," Marta scolded affectionately.

"No, she's not," Ben said. "I like my women on the slim side."

Stacey rose to the bait immediately. "I'm not your woman."

Ben cocked an eyebrow at her and stood up, his long body seeming to unfold endlessly from behind the table. "Not yet," he agreed easily.

"I could sell out," she reminded him, wishing he wouldn't stand over her like that. Even across the width of the table his great height and breadth of shoulder were intimidating.

He shrugged. "You could," he said. It took all his considerable self-control to appear unconcerned either way. "But you won't."

"You're awfully sure of yourself."

"Sure of you," he corrected. "I saw that greedy little gleam in those big blue eyes of yours. You want this ranch and all the goodies that go with it."

"I don't," she said, and stood to gain whatever advantage her height might give her. She still had to tilt her head a bit to meet his eyes. "I don't care about the money or the oil wells. I—"

"Am I to take that avaricious gleam to mean that you covet me, then?" he mocked softly.

Unaccountably Stacey blushed. She hadn't blushed for years, not since her teens, and even then, it would have taken more than a smart remark like that to make the color come rushing to her cheeks.

"This is my home," she said hotly, looking to Pete for support, but both he and the lawyer had risen when she did and were already backing away from the table.

Did nobody stand up to this bully?

She reached out toward her water glass, itching to fling its contents at his arrogant head. Something in his eyes stopped her, a quiet look, but dangerous nonetheless. She knew, beyond a doubt, that he wouldn't hesitate to retaliate, and with equal certainty, she knew that no one would stop him. Without a word being spoken, she allowed her hand to fall back to her side.

"Smart girl," he said with a wry twist of his mouth. And then he turned, following the other two men out the door, wondering just what he would have done if she hadn't backed down. And why in hell he'd pushed her to the point where she'd had to.

3

STACEY WAS LEFT STANDING openmouthed with impotent fury. "Damn him!" she swore softly.

How many times had he caused her to lose her temper today? Twice? Three times? However many, it was too many. And to think that she, renowned all over Paris for her cool head and icy control, hadn't said a hasty, unconsidered word in years. Probably not since the last time he'd goaded her beyond thinking rationally.

"Damn him." She hit her closed fist on the table in frustration. "Damn him, damn him!"

"Sit, sit." Marta pressed Stacey back into her chair with one hand, pouring her another cup of cinnamon-spiced coffee with the other.

"How can you all let him get away with it?" Stacey fumed. She reached for the narrow leather clutch purse that lay beside her napkin.

"It is his right." Marta didn't pretend to misunderstand. "He has been the *jefe* for a long time now. It is only natural that he should have the respect and obedience of those who live here, no?"

"What about my grandfather? He was the *jefe* of Iron Oakes last time I heard. Didn't he have any say? And Uncle Pete." She fingered the clasp on her gold cigarette case with one hand, opening and closing it. "Does Ben ride roughshod over him, too?"

"But, no, of course not!" Marta sounded shocked that Stacey would even suggest such a thing. "Benito rides rough over no one. And he takes nothing that is not his due." She began stacking plates on a wooden tray. "It is only that your grandfather was not a well man before he died and—"

"Henry was ill before he died? But I thought—" Stacey twisted around in her chair to look at Marta, the temptations of the cigarette case forgotten for the moment. "He was thrown, wasn't he?"

"*Sì*, from that painted devil of a horse. But he was old, *niña*," Marta said, her head bent over her task. "As Señor Pete is old. Old and tired and glad to lay the burden on younger shoulders." She lifted her head, her black eyes twinkling. "And such broad shoulders, no? Benito is much man, *muy hombre, sì?*"

"He's an overgrown, ill-mannered ox," Stacey said grumpily.

"Ah, pah! You are as stubborn as he is." Marta lifted the tray and headed toward the kitchen.

Stacey finished her coffee in solitude, one hand still fiddling with the cigarette case, opening and closing the gold clasp.

Nasty habit.

The words echoed through her mind and she wavered for another moment, torn between smoking just to score a point against Ben and her own good common sense. It was silly, she decided, to continue polluting her lungs just because she was mad at Ben. After all, she'd been mad at Ben for a good portion of the past eleven years and she was probably going to be even madder at him in the future. She left the cigarette case on the table and carried her empty coffee cup into the kitchen.

"That was a truly delicious meal, Marta," she said, hugging the housekeeper from behind. "You remembered all of my favorite dishes. Thank you."

The older woman took refuge in gruffness, pleased and embarrassed by Stacey's warm thanks. "Go to your room and rest. I have work to do." She waved her away with a soapy hand. "Go."

"I've rested enough." She squeezed Marta again, planting a smacking kiss on her cheek before she let her go. "I want to look around."

"Well, look somewhere else, then," Marta scolded her affectionately, "and do not clutter up my kitchen with your foolishness."

Stacey laughed lightly, happily. How many times in the past had Marta chased her from the kitchen for getting in the way? "I'll stay out of your way," she promised, turning to poke into the nooks and crannies of the big cozy room.

Changes had been made inside as well as out, she noted, the beginnings of trepidation tugging at her heartstrings. The old refrigerator had been replaced with a newer model, a dishwasher had been installed, and there was a big double oven in the adobe wall next to the stove. A food processor, as shiny new as if it had just come out of the box, sat on the tiled counter next to the old apple-shaped cookie jar.

"This is quite a machine," Stacey said, touching it lightly. "I'll bet it does everything but plant the crops."

"Ah, pah!" Marta shrugged, up to her elbows in sudsy dishwater, obviously unwilling to trust the fine crystal to the mercies of the new dishwasher.

Stacey smiled to herself, the trepidation beginning to fade. Some things might have changed but not Marta. Marta would always prefer the old, known ways no matter how many new appliances she had.

"Benito bought it," the housekeeper went on. "To save me work, he said. Pah! I only have more to clean."

But Stacey could tell that she was pleased. Not with the new appliances exactly, but with the evidence of Ben's care and concern. Stacey was feeling pretty pleased herself at the moment. Not with Ben's concern, of course, but with the realization that all the modern appliances hadn't taken away from the warm rustic charm of the kitchen she remembered so fondly from her childhood.

The rough-textured, white-washed walls were still the same as she remembered them, touched now with a golden glow by the late-afternoon sunlight streaming through the narrow arched doors that opened onto the courtyard. Marta's carved wooden crucifix still hung above the double doors that gave access to the dining room. The long trestle-style table still ran down the center of the kitchen, surrounded by eight ladderback chairs with woven cane seats.

Stacey ran her fingers over the scarred tabletop, engraved with the name of nearly everyone who had ever eaten in Marta's kitchen. Stacey's was there, several times over. And Ben's. She touched the entwined hearts and initials, hers and Ben's, that had been carved there so long ago. She had been nine or ten at the time, still young enough to cherish a severe case of hero-worship for the teenaged Ben, who had done it to please her.

Nostalgia welled up unexpectedly, filling her with a wistful longing for something that once was and could never be again. Foolish tears filled her eyes. She blinked them back. She was long past hero-worship, and Ben was no hero, anyway. He never had been. She brushed her eyes with the back of her hand. "I guess I'll go rest, after all," she said to Marta, saying the first thing that came to mind as she sidled past the housekeeper.

I'm just tired, Stacey told herself as she hurried through the dining room. *It's the time difference; jet lag; the fu-*

neral this morning. I am just tired! She sniffed determinedly, her steps slowing as she entered the living room.

It, too, had thick, whitewashed adobe walls. The ceilings were low and beamed. The furniture was mostly rich brown leather and oversize, as if it were intended for use by a race of giant men. Stacey smiled through the unshed tears that still shimmered in her eyes.

That was just the image, she thought, that Texas strived to give the rest of the world. Texans were supposed to be bigger, smarter, richer, more generous, more everything than anyone else. Their women were prettier, their horses—and cars—were faster and they drank their whiskey straight. Or so the legend went. Most Texans believed the legend and, from what Stacey had observed in her travels, it seemed that most of the rest of the world believed it, too. Everyone, it seemed, loved a cowboy. A Texas cowboy, in particular.

She wandered around the living room, which, like the kitchen, was chock-full of memories, full of family legends and stories and shared laughter, full of the girl she used to be. The girl she could never be again, she thought wistfully, even if she stayed.

If.

The thought startled her; she'd already made up her mind, hadn't she? Yes, she told herself. Yes, she had. She was home and she was staying. And to hell with the girl she used to be.

She didn't want to be that girl, anyway. That girl had been too highstrung and emotional, too vulnerable, too much in love with a man who'd turned out to be a lowdown snake. She was infinitely better off as she was now—especially when it looked as if she might be forced to marry that snake to keep what was hers.

And then, no, she thought in the next instant. She couldn't marry him. The idea was totally ridiculous. But she couldn't lose the ranch, either. Not again. Not ever again. Not even if she had to stand toe-to-toe with Ben Oakes and battle it out for the rest of her natural life.

THE LITTLE jeweled travel alarm buzzed somewhere near her head. Stacey jackknifed to a sitting position, reaching to silence it. She sat still for a moment, the clock cupped in her hands, listening for any sounds of stirring in the silent, sleeping house. There were none.

Satisfied that she had wakened no one else, Stacey put the clock back on the bedside table and swung her long legs out of bed. Aided only by the moonlight that streamed in through the louvered shutters, she slipped into her robe, belting it loosely over the matching silk nightgown that Marta had admired and, barefoot, made her way quietly from her room.

It was dark in the hall. She paused on the top of the stairs, letting her eyes adjust to the darkness before proceeding cautiously, one slow step at a time, down the wide, wooden staircase, automatically avoiding the fifth one from the top that had always creaked.

It was light again at the bottom of the steps, the moonlight shining softly through the glass doors that led out onto the courtyard. It cast its wavering shadows over the solid brown leather furniture, making the oversized chairs and sofa look eerily like large animals hunkered down for sleep.

Stacey shivered slightly, dismissing the thought, and walked toward the doors that led to the courtyard. Opening them, she stood in the night air with her arms wrapped around her middle. The sun had gone down hours ago and one might have expected it to have cooled off by now. But it hadn't. At least, not much. She'd almost forgotten how hot a summer's night in Texas could be. And how beautiful.

Without the clutter of neon signs and city streetlights to compete with, the night sky was an endless expanse of inky blackness lit by thousands upon thousands of tiny, twinkling stars and the bright lantern of a nearly full moon. It shone down, casting its ghostly light over the utter silence of the night and glimmering off the softly splashing water in the fountain in the center of the courtyard. Stacey sighed, hugging herself as she gazed up at the smiling face of the man in the moon. It had been just such a night when she'd taken her last moonlit ride on Iron Oakes's land.

It had been later in the summer, though, not quite so hot, and her companion had been a man. Not Ben who, newly graduated from college, seemed to have no time to spare for her then. And not one of the many boys of her own age who clamored around her that summer like eager bees around a new honeypot. Her companion that night had been an "older" man; in his midtwenties only, but older in comparison to Stacey's fifteen. A new employee not long on the ranch who either didn't know, or, more likely, didn't care, that the *jefe*'s pretty little granddaughter was off limits. Henry hadn't seemed to notice anything amiss, but Ben hadn't liked the attention the new hand paid to her.

"You're just a kid and he's too old for you," he'd said. "Keep away from him."

That was all it took. She'd snuck out one night—after carefully planting a note—to meet her admirer for a midnight ride with some vague idea of making Ben sit up and take notice of her newfound maturity. But her companion had wanted much more than the few innocent kisses Stacey had thought to exchange. When Ben finally caught up with them they were rolling around in the dust near a dying campfire, Stacey all undone and screaming with anger and fear. .

Ben had hauled the cowboy off of her with one hand. She'd scrambled away, unaware at first that she'd been rescued, and grabbed up a gnarled piece of mesquite wood to defend herself. But it was unnecessary. Ben had already hit him.

She could still remember the sickening sound of breaking bones as Ben's fist smashed savagely against the other man's nose. The second blow had sent the ranch-hand sprawling and in a low, dangerously controlled voice, Ben ordered him off Iron Oakes land. There had been a long, taut silence, she remembered, while the two men measured each other. Her assailant was older and more experienced at brawling, but Ben was bigger, much bigger, and a killing rage boiled in his steely blue eyes.

"Never did like a tease, anyhow," the cowboy said, wiping at the blood that trickled from his nose as he turned away. Only after he was gone, swallowed by the darkness, did Ben turn to Stacey. The look on his face scared her almost more than the attempted rape had done.

"Ben," she said, taking a step back. She lifted the makeshift mesquite wood club she was holding as if to ward him off, her knuckles white with the fierceness of her grip. "It wasn't—I didn't—"

"Don't say a word." He yanked the stick out of her hand and tossed it aside, then reached out and grabbed her by the wrists, shaking her slightly. She stumbled against him and his hands went automatically to her shoulders. He shook her again. "Just don't say a word. I don't want to hear it." He thrust her away from him with a gesture of disgust. "Get on your horse."

"Please, Ben." Her eyes filled. This wasn't how it was supposed to be at all! This wasn't how she'd planned it! He wasn't supposed to push her away in anger and disgust. He was supposed to hold her. Comfort her. Tell her he had never realized how much he loved her until this moment. But something had gone horribly wrong. She reached out to touch him, to placate and plead for understanding. "Please." Her hand touched the middle of his chest.

He went absolutely still.

She could feel his madly, erratically beating heart and the faint wetness of his sweat-dampened chambray shirt. His breathing was harsh and fast. Much faster than it should have been, even considering his mad ride and the thrashing he had just given her attacker.

Hope welled up as she recognized the emotion that gripped him. How many times over the years had Marta smacked her with one hand while holding her close with the other? He was angry because he loved her, that was all, she'd thought, relieved. Angry and afraid for what might have happened to her.

Oh, Ben, dear sweet Ben, her young heart cried out. *You do love me.*

Without conscious volition she moved a step nearer, her other hand reaching out to join the first. "It's all right," she crooned softly, stroking his heaving chest as if soothing a restive horse. "It's all right, Ben. He didn't hurt me. I'm all right."

He moved then, his big rawboned hands coming up to capture hers, pressing the palms flat against the hard, muscled wall of his chest.

"I'm so glad you came after me, Ben," she breathed, swaying toward him, believing that now, at last, the night would turn out as she'd intended it to. "So glad. I didn't mean—"

"No, you didn't mean it." His voice was strained and low. His hands tightened, crushing her fingers in his grasp. "You never mean it, do you? You strut around in those tight jeans with nothing on under your blouse. You wiggle and tease, just like he said, until some poor fool takes you up on it, but you don't mean it."

"Ben!" she said, aghast. What was he saying? Why was he blaming her? She hadn't meant for the man to attack her. "I didn't do anything!" she defended herself. "He tried—"

"He tried what? To take you up on what you offered? Can you blame him?" His eyes, hot, caressing, accusing, traveled over her disheveled form. He let go of one of her hands and reached out to run one callused fingertip over the upper curve of the high, young breast that was partially exposed by her torn shirt.

Stacey stood frozen, paralyzed by his delicate touch and the wondering, wanting, tortured look on his face.

"Could any man blame him?" Ben whispered raggedly, and then shook his head in answer to his own question. "I can't," he said. Both hands moved downward, lightly outlining her budding figure, coming to rest on her denim-sheathed hips. "I'd like to kill the bastard—" his fingers tightened, biting into her "—but I can't really blame him."

Stacey was scarcely aware of what he said, so intent was she on trying to read the expression on his face in the flickering shadows of the dying fire. What she saw there—or thought she saw there—only confused her more.

There was desire in his expression, yes. Even as inexperienced as she was, she could see that. But she could also see that he was fighting that desire. The battle was evident in the tightened line of his full lower lip and his clenched jaw and the pinched, strained look around his eyes. And overlaying it all was a disgust he didn't even try to hide. For her? Was he disgusted by what he'd thought she'd done?

"It wasn't like that, Ben," she said frantically. "Honest, it wasn't! I only rode out with him because you told me not to a-and—" it was so hard to say with him looking at her like that "—and so that you'd come after me," she finished in a small voice.

Ben's eyes flared wide for an instant. "You *wanted* me to come after you?"

"Yes." It was barely a whisper.

"Why?" Just that one word, and his eyes looking at her so strangely.

Didn't he know? she thought. Couldn't he see why?

"Because I...because..." But she couldn't tell him why, couldn't put into words what she felt now that she was given the chance. Not with him looking at her like that.

"Did you want me to kiss you, Stacey, like he did?" His fingers flexed on the curve of her hips. "Did you?"

She bit her lip and nodded once, hesitantly. This was what she wanted, wasn't it? This is what she had dreamed about for months now? Ben holding her. Ben about to kiss her. And yet...

"Say it, Stacey," he demanded roughly. "I want to make sure I understand you." His hands tightened, pulling her unresisting body to his. His breath was hot on her face. "Tell me you want me to kiss you."

"I..." But suddenly, standing there with her lower body held to the hardness of his and her hands flat against his heaving chest, she was no longer sure that's what she wanted at all. It hadn't been this way in her daydreams. When she'd thought about it, planned it, it had been all soft and pretty and filled with sweet, warm emotion. But there was nothing soft or pretty or sweet about this. This was all too real. And it was frightening. *He* was frightening.

"Changed your mind again?" he said when she hesitated. His voice was low, as dangerous as a coiled snake. "Decided you don't want me, either, now that it comes right down to it, is that it? All teasing and cute little games and we play by your rules or we don't play at all?" He brought one hand up to the back of her neck and curled his fingers into her long, tangled hair, forcing her head back. "What happens if I don't want to play by your rules? What if I just take what I want?" His eyes burned over her upturned face. Hard, implacable, terrifying eyes. "There's no one here to stop me like I stopped him."

Stacey whimpered and squeezed her eyes closed. She'd never seen this Ben before. Never even guessed that he existed inside the Ben she knew.

"Ben, don't." She arched away from him, pushing against his chest with both hands. It was like pushing against a stone wall. Panic knifed through her. "Please, don't." She lifted wide, tear-filled eyes to his. "Don't."

Their eyes held for a long, taut moment. They were both breathing hard, both tense and stiff, both waiting for what the other would do next. And then Ben shifted his hold and stooped, picking her up before she quite knew what had happened. Without another word he tossed her onto her horse and, with her reins in his hand, mounted his.

They rode back to the house in silence, Stacey being led like an irresponsible child. Two days later, Ben had confronted her grandfather with the accusation that she was "growing up wild" and together the two men had contrived to have her sent away.

Stacey sighed deeply, thinking vaguely of lost innocence and lost love, and brought her wandering mind back to the present. What was past was past, and she had more pressing things to attend to now. Such as her reason for being up in the middle of the night.

She'd set her alarm, taking into account the time difference, so that she could catch André in his Paris office the very first thing in the morning. She needed his advice because, sometime during the evening meal, which Ben never came in for, she'd decided that she was going to need a lawyer. André, with his far-flung oil empire, would know the best. And she was going to need the best if she was going to fight Henry's will and win.

She turned back inside, leaving her memories to float uneasily on the night air, and walked through the dark, sleeping house to her grandfather's den. With fifteen minutes to wait before she could be sure that André would be in his office, she poured herself a small brandy and curled up in the big leather chair she'd occupied just that morning. Sipping her drink in the warm, cocooning darkness, she tried to tell herself that, no, she didn't want a cigarette. Five futile minutes later, she sighed and straightened, reaching for the battered silver box that Henry had always kept full of his own special brand of smokes. *Just one*, she solemnly promised herself, lifting the lid.

The box was full of sour lemon candies.

Making a small sound of annoyance, she sat her drink on the wide arm of the chair and rose to move behind the desk, reaching for the lids of the other small boxes lined up above the leather ink blotter. She found stamps, rubber bands, paper clips and loose change but no cigarettes.

Well, damn, she thought, lifting file folders and loose papers as her search became more frantic. *Henry always had cigarettes. He'd smoked like the proverbial chimney.* Getting desperate as only a quitting smoker can, she reached out and snapped on the small, green-shaded desk lamp to aid her search.

4

RUBBING ABSENTLY at the back of his neck, Ben walked past the row of box stalls, turning off the bright overhead lights as he went. He was hot and tired and sweaty, his neck and upper back aching from the long struggle to help Lone Star deliver her first foal. Because of the mare's extreme nervousness and the added difficulty of a breech birth, he and the vet had nearly lost them both a couple of times. But mother and baby were doing fine now and the Iron Oakes Stable had another potential winner in the awkward, spindly-legged newborn who'd already managed to struggle to her feet for her first meal.

The thought gave Ben a great deal of satisfaction, beyond that of helping a new life safely into the world, because the addition of a racing stable to the Iron Oakes holdings had been his idea. And it was proving to be a good one.

He turned off the last light and pushed open the wide door, stepping out of the barn and into the dark, star-studded night. He headed down the well-worn path to the main house, his sense of satisfaction fading a bit with every step, replaced by a curious mix of feelings made up of wariness and irritation, anger and affection, and something he could only label as nostalgia. Nostalgia brought on by the very natural reminiscing about the past that was part of mourning and—*might as well face it*, he thought—the fact that Stacey had finally come home.

Ah, Stacey.

She'd been the kid sister that he'd never had, an occasional tag-along pest, a preadolescent who'd liked loud music and bright colors. And, finally, a temptation.

It'd been on a night much like this one—still, starry, hot—that he'd finally realized they couldn't go on as they had been that summer so long ago when she'd turned from little girl to woman. Together too much, alone too often.

After that night, he'd deliberately set about convincing Henry that she needed to be sent away for her own good. For his good, too, he admitted, because, naively, he'd thought that the distance would cure him of his unholy craving for her.

It didn't, of course, especially after Marta had finally told him that his desire for Stacey wasn't as unholy as he'd feared. It was time that finally did the trick. Lots of time. For three years, he'd continued to think about her. Despite the anger she'd spewed at him, despite the lack of letters besides those she wrote to Marta, despite everything, he'd thought about how it would be when she finally came home and he could claim her as he wanted to. And he was sure she still wanted him to, under all the hurt feelings and injured pride.

Only she didn't.

Because, when her schooling was complete, she didn't come home. Not even for a visit. His first reaction had been to go to Paris and drag her back by the hair. His next inclination had been to let her rot over there, and good riddance! In the end, he hadn't gone after her and she, perversely, hadn't rotted. And with more time and the wisdom that comes with growing older and realizing that lust won't kill you, the desire had died a natural death.

He'd even begun to think of her as a sister he'd once been close to but had grown apart from.

And now she was home. It'd taken threats and tears and shouting to get her to leave Iron Oakes in the first place; it had taken the death of her grandfather to bring her back.

Would she stay now that she was here? This morning in Henry's office, she'd said she would. No, he thought, grinning into the night, she'd gotten good and mad and *threatened* to stay—and marry him if she had to. His grin faded.

"Dammit, Henry," he said to the sky. "Why the hell did you do it? At least you could've told me what you were planning."

He could have prepared himself then, somehow, to deal with it and all the conflicting emotions it had caused. As it was, well . . . He'd prepared himself to be pleasant and overlook his anger at her prolonged absence—the perfectly justified anger he felt on Henry's behalf. He'd been prepared to be magnanimous and forgive her neglect of her home and her aging grandfather.

But she'd walked into the front hall, as cool as you please, and looked around with all the icy disdain of a queen visiting a peasant's hovel. The first words out of her mouth had been a challenge! And she hadn't even sounded Texan! For some reason, that alone made him want to wring her beautiful neck.

He hadn't even known about the will then.

He kicked open the courtyard gate with the toe of his boot, guiltily catching it before it slammed against the adobe brick wall, and shut it behind him, angry with himself for allowing such a stupid, insignificant thing as a French accent to bother him when he had so many other, more important things he could be bothered about instead.

Oh, hell, face it, he thought, unbuttoning his shirt as he headed toward the courtyard fountain, it wasn't the accent that bothered him. He cupped his hands, splashing water over his heated face and chest. It was what that French accent represented. Stacey's long absence from Iron Oakes. Stacey's neglect. Stacey's life in Paris. Stacey's—

His thoughts broke off abruptly as a light came on in Henry's office. He straightened, absently wiping his face with the hem of his shirt, his eyes on the desk lamp glowing between the open curtains of the office.

Speak of the devil, he thought.

Stacey.

She was wearing some sort of movie-queen nightgown, all silk and sleekness in a soft ivory color. Her hair fell to her shoulders, slightly crinkled from the braid she'd worn all day. Her motions as she rummaged through the desk were quick. Almost frantic.

What in hell is she doing in Henry's office at—he glanced at his watch—*two-thirty in the morning?*

He took a deep breath and ran his hand through his damp hair, pushing it back, then strode silently, eagerly, across the courtyard and entered the unlatched patio door to Henry's office. "Can I help you find something?"

Stacey jumped as if she'd been scalded. The folder she was holding slid from her fingers, scattering papers across the desk. She reached out with both hands, snatching at them, squinting into the shadows beyond the light cast by the lamp as she stuffed them back into the folder. "Ben?"

He didn't move, didn't say anything else beyond those first accusation-tinged words, but she knew it was Ben. His height and the massiveness of his shoulders, even if he hadn't spoken at all, would have been identification enough.

"Ben," she said again, hating the vaguely guilty catch in her voice. She wasn't doing anything wrong, but it felt as if she was and looked that way, too, she was sure. "I didn't realize anyone else was still up," she offered and knew immediately that it was the wrong thing to say.

"Obviously," came the mocking reply. He walked into the room then, moving with deceptively lazy grace, and sank into the leather chair Stacey had vacated a few minutes earlier. One hand absently rubbed the back of his neck as he continued to watch her. What the hell was she doing, searching through Henry's desk?

Stacey stared back at him just as silently—as calm as a cool mountain lake on the outside, as agitated as a bubbling caldron of hot oil on the inside—waiting for whatever he would say next.

His faded denim workshirt was wet along the edges, hanging loose and open over his muscular torso. His black hair was disheveled, its slight tendency to curl more pronounced with the water that dampened it. And even across the width of the desk he smelled faintly of hay and horses and hardworking man.

The unbidden memory of another time, another night, when he'd looked like that, smelled like that, slipped into her mind, perhaps because she'd so recently been thinking of it. *Is his heart beating like a drum*, she wondered, and then frantically pushed the unwelcome thought away. She didn't want to be reminded or to know. Not now. Not ever.

"I'm sorry if I disturbed you." She knew she hadn't, but good manners—and her screaming nerves—demanded she say something to break the silence that stretched between them.

"I'm sure you are," he agreed. His eyes, those bottomless blue eyes, seemed to mock the inanity of her remark.

"How's the new foal?" she asked, remembering that Uncle Pete had mentioned that Ben was assisting at a difficult delivery.

"Just fine," Ben said, wondering why he didn't just ask her what she was looking for. "Lone Star took her own sweet time tonight, but both she and the new filly are doing fine."

"It was a long labor, wasn't it?" One hand moved aimlessly, fingering each item on the desk's surface.

"It was a breech birth." His eyes followed her wandering hand.

She stilled it, clasping it at her waist with the other. "Oh?"

"We had to turn the foal twice before she finally stayed turned." He sighed and rubbed the back of his neck again, as if trying to ease an ache.

Stacey surprised herself with a vague longing to move behind him and take over for his massaging hand. He looked so tired. So weary and—

"What are you looking for?" he asked abruptly.

The longing to soothe him died just as abruptly. "A cigarette," she said quickly. Too quickly, she thought, and a bit defensively. She could almost hear the apology in her voice. Damn! She had nothing to apologize for. "Couldn't find one, though," she said, shrugging, her voice purposely careless. "Henry give up cigarettes in his old age?" she asked lightly, almost jokingly, in a further effort to erase the apologetic-sounding words.

Ben's head snapped up, his massaging hand stilled at the back of his neck, his blue eyes dark with sudden anger. "He had to quit." His eyes bored into hers. "Doctor's orders."

"Doctor's orders?" she said, momentarily confused by Ben's unexpected anger and the shadow of pain in his eyes.

He stared at her for a long moment before answering, trying to determine if she was really as heartless as she sounded. The Stacey of old had been headstrong and quick to anger but not heartless. Never heartless. He didn't know what this new cool, cosmopolitan, Frenchified Stacey was. It was time, he decided, that he found out.

"He had cancer, Stacey," he said bluntly, his voice gone flat and nearly toneless. He ignored her small shocked gasp and the fluttering of one hand in a vague gesture of denial. "Lung cancer. He was dying slowly, day by agonizing day, of lung cancer. And *that's* why he gave up cigarettes in his old age!"

"I didn't know," Stacey found her voice with difficulty. It was thin and reedy. "I— Your telegram said he was thrown."

"From a horse that should never have been able to toss him. Wouldn't have, if he'd been a well man. But he was sick and in pain. Constant pain, I think, toward the end, though he'd never admit it. Old 'Iron' Oakes! Had to live up to his image." He gave a short bark of harsh, mirthless laughter and picked up Stacey's forgotten glass, tossing down the fiery liquid in one swallow.

"His image killed him," he said reflectively, more to himself than to her. "He wouldn't slow down, wouldn't check into the hospital for any more treatments after the first operation. Said he didn't want any more days than God saw fit to give him."

"Operation?" she echoed faintly. When had Henry had an operation? And why hadn't anyone told her about it?

"Said he wasn't going to die in some damned hospital bed," Ben continued as if he hadn't heard her, "hooked up to some damned machine. He wanted to go fast, with his damned boots on," he added, his voice husky with pain. He sat silently for a few minutes, gazing into the empty glass as if wondering where the drink had gone. "Well, he did that, didn't he?" he said finally, but Stacey hadn't heard him.

Her eyes were closed tightly against the hot tears that threatened to fall, trying to block out the image of her grandfather as sick and frail and dying. He'd always been such a powerful man. Not nearly as big as Ben but barrel chested and ham fisted, full of grandiose schemes and plans that he mostly made come true. He'd been so full of tenacious life, she thought, and their parting had been so angry, their last words so full of accusation and rage.

She remembered suddenly, with sharp, cruel clarity, the faces at the funeral, the condemnation in all those eyes and the way they slid away from hers. It wasn't just that she hadn't shed any tears at Henry's graveside. It was because they all thought she'd known that her grandfather was dying of cancer and hadn't bothered to come home until he was dead. Like a vulture, arriving in time for her share of the spoils.

Damn Henry for not telling her! And damn Ben for telling her now, this way!

"No one told me," she whispered hoarsely. "No one wrote. Marta's letters..." Her voice broke and she paused, struggling to control it. "She never said Henry was sick."

"Would you have cared?" His voice cut into her like a knife.

Stacey's eyes flew open. "Cared! Of course I cared! He was my grandfather! No matter what you think. In spite of everything, I...I loved him." She whirled away, turning her back to him, too proud to allow him to see the tears that finally escaped her control and slid slowly down her cheeks. She stood as straight and stiff as she had at the funeral, as she had that morning at the reading of the will. She wouldn't let them—Henry, Ben, any of them!—see how badly they could still hurt her.

Ben stared at her for a long moment. Her back was ramrod straight, but her shoulders were trembling under the shimmering material of her robe, a sure sign that she was crying.

"Dammit all to hell," he swore softly. He'd never been able to cope with her tears, especially if he'd been the one to cause them. They made him feel helpless and mean. Leather creaked as he rose from the chair. "Stacey..." He came around the desk and put a hand on her shoulder, urging her to turn to him. "I didn't mean to make you cry," he said, sounding weary and resigned, feeling guilty. "Stacey, honey, please don't cry."

She stiffened and pulled away, keeping her back to him, unwilling, as always, for anyone to see her tears. "I'm not crying," she said and sniffed.

"All right," he agreed, forcibly turning her into his arms. "You're not crying."

She stood stiffly for a second or two longer, trying to freeze him out, trying to hate him, but his hand went to her hair, gently stroking, and suddenly she was ten years old and he was the Ben he'd been then. Her friend, her protector, her whole world. She burrowed her face into his bare damp chest and sobbed as if her heart were breaking.

Ben comforted her as best he could, smoothing the fine golden-blond hair, whispering meaningless, consoling words, holding her as he'd once held a hurt child, letting her cry it all out.

And she did.

She cried for the scared fifteen-year-old, alone in Paris and too stubborn to cry for herself. She cried for the homesick career girl, too proud to come home without an invitation. She cried for the woman whose grandfather hadn't allowed her a proper farewell.

"Why didn't you tell me?" she asked when, at last, she could speak again. Her voice was muffled against his chest. "I would have come home, Ben. Nothing could have kept me away, if I'd known. Nothing."

She could feel his cheek against the top of her head and she thought she felt his lips move, but he said nothing in reply, just held her, one hand still gently, absently stroking her hair.

It was imperative, suddenly, that he believe her, that he understand. She could take everyone else thinking she was a cold, selfish bitch, but not Ben. She needed to hear him say that, despite what everyone else thought, he didn't think she was so small and hard-hearted that she wouldn't have come home if she had known that her grandfather really needed her.

"I would have come back, Ben," she said again, her hands flat against his chest now, pushing a little away from him to look up anxiously. Her eyes were soft and pleading. Her cheeks were tear streaked.

"Yes," he said softly, the word neither a confirmation nor a denial. He stopped his mindless stroking of her hair, moving his hand so that his palm lay against the side of her neck under the heavy curtain of her tumbled blond waves. Splaying his fingers against the base of her skull, he pressed her head back into his chest. He couldn't take her looking at him that way, all soft and vulnerable and pleading. It made him feel . . . too much. Remember too much.

Stacey resisted the pressure of his hand, refusing to be so easily comforted. "I would have, Ben," she insisted again, her voice barely above a whisper. She searched his face for a sign that he believed her. "I would."

"Yes," he said again. She was so beautiful, staring up at him like that! Her eyes were bluer than he remembered, their color intensified by emotion, shimmering beneath her tears, like bluebonnets after a spring rain. "Stacey," he murmured pleadingly, trying to push her head back down to his chest before she could see the heat that flickered in his own eyes. Heat and hunger and the awareness of a memory. "Stacey, honey, please."

She stilled in his arms, knowing exactly what he was remembering because, suddenly, she was remembering it, too.

It was that long-ago night all over again, she thought, staring up at him, except now they were starting where they'd left off. She could feel the passion growing in him, in his hand at her head and in the tenseness of his big body. And, like the last time, she was afraid. But afraid now of where and, more important, who they were. She wasn't fifteen anymore and crazy in love with a teenager's dream, and this was a Ben she no longer knew or, she told herself fiercely, even wanted to know. She stiffened, looking down, trying to pull away, but she'd hesitated too long.

Even as he warned himself not to, even as he told himself he was making a mistake, Ben tightened his fingers on the back of her neck and drew her closer. His other hand slid from her shoulder to the small of her back.

Stacey pushed his bare chest with the flat of both hands, but that served only to press her lower body more fully against him. She could feel the rock hardness of his denim-clad thighs against her own softness, could feel the buckle of his belt pressed against her abdomen. It was wonderful and it was frightening and it—

"Be still," he commanded softly, pushing her chin up with his thumb. The fingers still splayed along the back of her neck tightened, holding her head immobile. His hand on her back pressed her close.

Stacey squeezed her eyes closed. Her hands clenched into fists against his chest, pushing.

"Look at me," he demanded. The hand at her head tightened fractionally when she refused. "Stacey, look at me."

Her eyes flared wide, reflecting fear and defiance and arousal all at once, the icy disdain she'd so carefully cultivated forgotten. Their eyes, blue boring into blue, locked and held, exchanging heat and anger, years of resentment and hurt and desperate need. Against her will, she felt her resistance melting away as the flicker of memory in his eyes became a blue flame, devouring her.

"No," she managed to say, whether to him or to her own suddenly raging libido she didn't know, couldn't tell.

"No," she said as he bent his head toward hers. Her voice was weaker this time. Her hands against his chest lost all resistance, unclenching to curl sensuously in the damp, clinging black hairs. His heart *was* beating like a drum, she realized.

"Oh, no." It was a last, almost silent plea, but her lips were parted, a perfect O of instinctive invitation and Ben's mouth covered hers, taking her past her fears, past the present and into that night more than eleven years ago when all she'd ever wanted was him.

She felt herself give helplessly against him as he staggered back against the desk. Her whole body softened as if any remaining resistance, any lingering defiance, were being drained away at the touch of his lips on hers. She could feel as separate, distinct impressions the short crisp hairs on his chest curling damply around her now passive fingers, the large hand, warm and firm, against the small of her back, the strength of his hard-muscled inner thighs pressing against the outside of hers. She breathed in the musky, thoroughly welcome, male smell of him and pressed closer, burrowing into the notch of his splayed legs.

He groaned, deep in his chest, and the hand on her back shifted, moving lower to caress her bottom and press her more fully against his aching erection. Stacey gave up all coherent thought then, giving way to the glorious, overwhelming onslaught of pure, primal feeling.

Her mouth opened willingly under his. Her hands slid mindlessly up over his chest and shoulders to twine themselves in the damp, curling hair at his nape. Her body collapsed onto his, *into* his, as boneless and pliant as a rag doll.

He moved his hand again, gliding up her slim torso to brush the side of one silk-covered breast. She shifted slightly, bringing her breast more fully under his hand. He shuddered against her, like a man mortally wounded, and kneaded the soft, full flesh that overflowed his palm.

"Stacey." Her name, whispered against her open lips, tasted hot and honey sweet. "Oh, Stacey." His callused fingers probed gently, feverishly, for the opening in her robe.

She turned her body, instinctively allowing him freer access to what he sought. His hand slipped eagerly inside the robe and came up against the frail barrier of her silk nightgown. Stacey could have screamed with frustration. She wanted, desperately, to feel his hand on her bare, yearning flesh. He could have torn her nightgown then and she wouldn't have cared, probably wouldn't have even noticed, if it would have given her what she wanted.

But he didn't tear it. One finger found the V of her gown and followed it upward, over her chest and the inner swell of her breast, to her shoulder. Then his hand slid under the narrow strap, pushing it and the robe downward to bare a smooth rounded shoulder. And still downward, gently forcing one upraised arm from around his neck to hang limply at her side so that it was bared past the elbow and one full white breast was exposed, its rosy tip hardened and straining for his touch. But still Ben moved slowly, agonizingly slowly, not touching her bare flesh until Stacey's nerves were taut with desire and her nipple was swollen with need.

He'd waited so long for this, he thought feverishly, so long, and he wanted it to last forever. His lips left her mouth, planting hot, frantic, moist kisses along her jaw and down her throat and across her smooth bared shoulder.

Stacey's head fell back and she writhed against him, pressing into him, wanting him to please, please, *please*, touch her. He murmured something hot and arousing as his mouth found her ear and then his wet tongue probed gently inside, imitating the act they were both dying for.

Stacey moaned and then moaned again as his hand finally closed over her bared breast. He rolled the aching nipple between his thumb and forefinger, making the ache deeper and more intense, driving her desire higher than it had ever gone before.

"I want you, Stacey. Lord, how I want you!" he growled against her ear.

Wordlessly, mindlessly, she pushed her breast into his caressing hand wanting more, wanting everything, because this—as wonderful as it was—just wasn't enough. It had never been enough, she thought. Would never be enough.

He shifted his hand on her back, tightening it around her waist, and drew her up against his body until her toes were just barely touching the floor. She could feel him trembling against her, like a leaf clinging desperately to a limb, buffeted by strong winds. His mouth left off tormenting her ear and he bent, twisting his big body slightly, to take the swollen bud of her breast into his mouth. He sucked gently, seductively, greedily at the hardened pink nipple.

Stacey began to make soft whimpering sounds in her throat. Her arm tightened around his neck. Her back arched to bring him even closer. Her previously limp hand moved, trying to insinuate itself between their locked bodies, reaching for his belt buckle.

"Wait. Stacey, honey," he breathed against her burning flesh. "Not here. Wait." He lifted her as if she weighed no more than a feather and carried her into the shadowed hall and up the dark staircase to her room.

5

SHE HAD A BRIEF MOMENT of panic when he set her down in her girlhood bedroom. But his lips claimed hers again and his hand covered her breast and the panic disappeared as if it had never been.

He backed away after a long sweet moment and pushed the silk robe and gown off of her other shoulder, down to her waist so that both breasts were bared. The robe fell to the floor in a shimmering pool at her feet, but the nightgown clung at her hips. She stood there, trembling in the moonlight that streamed in through the half-open louvered doors, her arms and waist and shoulders looking far too fragile for the lush ripeness of her white breasts. Her rich, golden hair was tousled and wild from his hands. Her lips were swollen from his kisses. Her eyes were narrowed and glazed with a passion meant for him alone.

"Stacey," he breathed on a ragged sigh. "Oh, Stacey."

Gently, almost reverently, he reached out and placed a hand over each breast, carefully, so that the pink crests were pressed against the center of his palms and his fingers were splayed over the full upper slopes. He stood there like that for a moment, his eyes closed, not moving, not speaking, just touching her, his thumbs brushing softly over the inner swell of her breasts. And then, his eyes still closed, his face rigid with passion, he began to move his hands over her body—feverishly, frantically—tracing the curves of her shoulders and arms and waist and breasts with his palms. The frenzied caress left trails of fire flickering along her skin and stoked the hot flame of her desire into a raging inferno of need.

"You're so beautiful," he said gruffly, his eyes opening at last. The fire that burned in hers blazed tenfold in his. "I always knew you would be." He drew a deep, unsteady breath. "I dreamed you would be."

She reached out then, wanting to touch him, too, wanting to give him as much pleasure as he was giving her. She ran her long salmon-pink nails lightly over his chest, scraping over his flat male nipples, tugging the dark, crinkly hairs that blurred the definition of his work-honed muscles.

Ben stood very still, his chest pumping like a bellows, watching her face as her hands traveled upward over his massive shoulders. Palms flat, fingers curved against his skin, she slipped them under the opened shirt and down his hard-muscled arms, leaving the damp chambray in a heap on the floor.

She moved toward him then, a small half step to close the little space between them as she reached for his belt buckle. Her foot caught in the tangle of material at their feet and she stumbled. Her breasts flattened against his bare chest. Her outstretched hands pressed against the bulging fly of his jeans.

Something in him snapped, a letting go of whatever slim control he'd been holding on to, and his hands, instead of righting her, toppled her backward onto the bed. With feverish haste he stripped off the rest of his clothes and then dragged Stacey's silk nightgown down off her hips, throwing it carelessly to the floor as his weight pressed her into the bed.

"Stacey." He breathed her name again, over and over, as if to reassure himself that the woman he held was the one he had dreamed about. His hands were everywhere on her body—touching her face and throat and breasts, contouring her belly and thighs, stroking the growing moistness between her legs—until she began to whimper again, softly, deep in her throat. Her body arched in silent supplication, her back lifting from the bed in mindless, aching need.

"Yes, that's it, honey," he panted against her neck. "Yes, right now. I can't wait any longer, either." His words were almost inaudible as he positioned himself over her body. "I've waited so long already," he murmured, opening her thighs even wider with the pressure of his knees. "So long."

But Stacey was past listening to what he said. She heard only the need and desire in his voice, a need and desire that matched her own. Her hands clutched his arms, pulling him to her, and she wrapped her long legs strongly around his hips. Her body arched instinctively, offering herself to him, poised to take whatever he would give.

Ben slipped his hands under her hips, lifting her even higher against him, and took what she offered. Took it feverishly, hungrily, as she gave it. Their bodies moved in a fierce, primitive rhythm for long moments, accompanied by the sounds of his harsh, hurried breathing and Stacey's low moans of pleasure. The muffled thud of flesh striking flesh filled the air around them as their hips came together again and again, faster and then faster still, driving them relentlessly toward the culmination of long-denied desire. And then Stacey stiffened beneath him, hit by an ecstasy so sharp and intense that she cried out his name. Her nails dug into his buttocks as she clung to him with all her strength. He found his release a heartbeat later, a ragged groan of deep satisfaction rumbling up from his chest as his big body tightened like a bow above her.

"Stacey," he sighed. "Stacey." He lowered his chest to hers, wrapping his arms tightly around her, and buried his face in the tangled hair at her neck.

They lay like that for long moments without speaking, their breathing slowly returning to normal, still locked in the closest embrace possible between a man and a woman until Ben finally rolled away from her, onto his side, and propped himself up on one elbow to look down into her flushed face.

Shyly, now that passion was spent, Stacey looked away, unsure of what she might see in his eyes, of what he might see in hers. Now that the reckless, primitive, desperately needy feeling was past and they were two separate people again, she felt curiously defenseless. Curiously alone.

It was as if she'd made too fast a transition in time from the here and now to the past and back again with no time to adjust or evaluate. It had all happened so fast. Everything, all her feelings, had merged for that brief, breathless time; all the love and hate she'd ever felt for Ben, all the anger and hurt, her grief at her grandfather's death and her joy at being home had all tumbled together so that she couldn't tell one from the other. She needed time to sort it all out, time to understand what it all meant, to understand how she felt. She needed, suddenly, to be alone.

Lying there by her side, watching the conflicting emotions chase across her face, Ben could almost feel her slipping away from him. He had to fight the crazy impulse to grab her and hold on tight. "I'm glad that's settled," he said, compelled to bring her back from wherever it was she'd gone.

Stacey turned her head to look up at him. The moonlight filtered through the long shuttered doors, casting dark slanted shadows like some old black and white movie across his face that made it unreadable. She could see his mouth clearly, but that was all.

"Glad what's settled?" she asked.

"Henry's will." Uncertainty warred with the note of sexual satisfaction in his voice. He struggled to overcome it. "We can drive to Lubbock tomorrow and get married."

"Married?" she said very carefully.

"There's no sense wasting any time over it now the decision's been made." He shrugged. "If you really want to, though, I guess it could wait until next week. Marta could arrange some sort of shindig. She'd get a real kick out of it." He stared down at her as he spoke, carefully not touching her, wishing to hell he could read what was going on behind those too-cool blue eyes of hers. They were shuttered now. Guarded. Not begging for his understanding, not shooting sparks of angry defiance, not half-closed with passion and promise. Not anything. She'd been so open, so giving, a moment ago, so much the old Stacey, and now she was . . . Hell, he didn't know *what* she was! Couldn't tell what she wanted.

But if it came right down to it, he didn't know what the hell he wanted, either. Marriage? Did he really want a marriage that'd been dictated by some ornery old wildcatter's will? Or was it just the old guilt raising its ugly head now that he'd gone and done what he'd once been sure would send him straight to hell? Was it really possible that he was thinking of going along with Henry's last wishes because he'd finally bedded Stacey—inviolate, untouchable Stacey—and now he felt he had to marry her? Was that it?

"But if we're going to wait until next week," he said, looking for a way out of the hole he'd dug for himself, "we might as well wait two or three." He shrugged uneasily at the questioning look in her eyes. "I've got two more mares about to foal any day now and—"

Stacey sat up abruptly, turning her back on him, and reached for her robe on the floor. Now that he'd gotten what he'd wanted all along, the lousy, low-down snake was having second thoughts, she thought indignantly, conveniently forgetting that she was having a few second—and third and fourth—thoughts of her own. Just who in the hell did he think he was?

She stood up and shrugged into the robe without a word. The need to be alone, to put some space between them, wasn't just a feeling now, it was an overwhelming urgency. She had to have some space to think, had to decide what this meant to her, what she wanted to do about it. Until then, she wasn't giving anything away. Certainly not any rash promises of marriage, and certainly not to Ben. She tightened the sash on the robe with a savage tug and turned to look down at him. "What makes you think we're getting married?" she said acidly.

He lay very still on the bed, staring up at her. "You made me think we're getting married," he said stubbornly, despite his own doubts about the wisdom of such words. His voice was low, careful, clipped. "Just now."

"Really, Ben." Stacey forced a laugh into her voice. "You're as medieval as Henry's will." She moved toward the dresser as she spoke and picked up a silver-backed hairbrush. "Just because two people go to bed together doesn't mean they're getting married," she said, vigorously brushing her hair as she watched him in the mirror. He still hadn't moved. "Not even in Texas."

"We're not just any two people."

"No." She put the brush down and turned to face him, crossing her arms as she leaned back on the dresser. "We're related. Uncle and niece, remember?"

Ben flinched as if she'd taken a swing at him. That old bugaboo would *not* cause him any more guilt! "Not by blood."

"Maybe." She shrugged, looking very French as she made the gesture. "Maybe not."

Incensed, and not quite sure why, Ben sat up abruptly and reached for his jeans. "You don't believe that any more than I do," he said through clenched teeth, wondering why the hell he didn't just take the out she'd handed him instead of arguing about it. Or tell her the truth, just as Marta had told him eleven years ago. "Henry wouldn't have put that clause in his will if we were related by blood."

Stacey's eyebrows rose. "Wouldn't he?"

He stood, zipping his jeans, and then faced her, his hands planted firmly on his lean hips. "You know damned well he wouldn't!" he snapped. His eyes bored into hers, turning the full force of his steely gaze on her.

Stacey drew herself up, refusing to be intimidated by him. "No, I *don't* damn well know it!" Her eyes blazed back at him with an equally fierce light. "I haven't got the faintest idea what Henry would or wouldn't do. I hadn't seen him for eleven years, remember? For all I know he could have been senile."

Ben took a menacing half step toward her.

Stacey lifted her chin, refusing to back down, and tossed her head disdainfully, daring him to . . . to something! "Judging by that will of his I'd say he was definitely senile, or damn close to it!"

They were speaking in tense, angry whispers, both of them well aware of the need to keep their argument—and all that had gone before it—quiet.

"Stacey, I'm warning you." He reached out with one hand and grasped her upper arm, giving her a little shake, wondering just what in hell he was warning her about.

Stacey's chin lifted even higher, haughty as an affronted queen. "You don't scare me, cowboy." She didn't even acknowledge the hand on her arm. "There's nothing you can do that would scare me."

Ben shook her again. "What I ought to do is whale the tar out of you," he threatened, frustrated beyond thinking.

"That won't get you what you want."

"Which is?"

"My agreement to Henry's will." All sexual passion between them was forgotten as she glared up at him, her eyes as fiery blue as his. "And full ownership of this ranch without having to pay for it. I know that's what you want, that that's why you—" she faltered slightly "—why you took me to bed just now. You thought I'd just lie back and say yes, didn't you? Well, I won't."

Ben threw both hands up. "Dammit, Stacey, the will didn't have anything to do with—" he waved a hand at the rumpled bed "—that."

"No?" She crossed her arms. "Then what did?"

Good question, he thought. *What did?* "Hell, I don't know. Propinquity? Shared grief? The need to reaffirm life in the face of death? Curiosity about what it would be like after all these years?" He ran a hand through his hair. "How the hell do I know?"

"How about greed?" she suggested.

"Greed?" He knew he'd been . . . hungry. But greedy? Had she thought he'd been a greedy lover?

"Yes, greed," she said. "As in yours for everything that Henry had. But you're not going to get it, Ben, because no matter what you do, seduce me or beat me, I'm still going to fight you on this. And I'll win, too. You see if I don't," she challenged. "I'm not one of your sweet little West Texas girls anymore, Ben, and I've—"

"Sweet?" he scoffed. "When were you ever sweet?"

"—grown up," she went on, ignoring his sarcasm, "and I won't bow down to the *jefe* of Iron Oakes like some insipid Southern belle simply because he orders it." She poked him in the chest with her finger. "I don't take orders from anyone, Ben. Not anymore."

He stared down at her for a second longer, his jaw clenched, the little pulse in his temple beating furiously as he fought for self-control, wondering how the hell they had got from the passionate embrace on her bed to this equally passionate anger. Wondering, too, why the hell it excited him so. "You turned into a real bitch while you were away," he said at last, needing to say something.

Stacey smiled nastily. "And I've got you to thank for that, don't I?"

Ben raised his hand as if to take her arm again but instead, he made a low sound in his throat, like a growl, and turned away from her. In one quick motion he bent over to scoop up his boots and the rest of his clothes from the floor and headed for the door. "You can't win," he said, pausing in the doorway. "There's no way in hell you can win."

"We'll see," she said, holding her ground until he turned and left the room.

When he was gone, all the emotion in the room seemed to have gone with him. She sagged back against the front of the dresser, wrapping her arms protectively around her middle. Well, she was alone, as she'd wanted to be, but something was wrong. Terribly wrong. She felt betrayed and deserted, somehow, just as she had when they'd sent her to Paris all those years ago. Tears shimmered on her cheeks.

Oh, Ben, she thought, *how can you do this to me? And, how could I have allowed you to*—her mind faltered, not knowing what to call what had passed between them there on the bed. It certainly hadn't been lovemaking—*to do what you did?*

Because there was no getting around it—she *had* allowed it. Had allowed it willingly, had even acted the aggressor when he wasn't moving fast enough to suit her. Ben hadn't used any force. He had, in fact, seemed to be acting under the same sort of mindless compulsion as she'd been. A mindless compulsion that had driven them into each other's arms—and then set them at each other's throats.

Sighing, she crossed the room and dropped on the edge of the bed, running a hand over sheets still warm from their entwined bodies.

Perhaps they'd both just been acting out the memory of a night long ago. Perhaps they'd just finally expressed something that should have been expressed between them years ago and then forgotten.

Resolutely, Stacey straightened her back and dried her tears. She was through crying. She'd shed all the tears she was going to, for her grandfather, for herself and for Ben. She would fight Ben for the ranch, and Pete and Marta, too, if she had to. It was her right. She was, after all, Henry "Iron" Oakes's only blood relative. That should count for something.

With a determined toss of her head, she stood and started back downstairs to her grandfather's office. She still had to call André and get the name of a good lawyer.

6

STACEY AWOKE the next morning heavy eyed and un-rested and lay tiredly for a moment, staring blankly at the ceiling, debating whether it was worth it to get up.

André had been more than helpful last night when she finally called him. He gave her the name of a Dallas law-yer, Lyle Higgins, who, he said, had handled a few things for him over the years when Edouard had gone to school in Texas and he—André—had always been most satis-fied with the results.

"We are missing you very much, *chérie*," he said warmly after he'd given her the information she re-quested. "Edouard does not know which of his ends is up. He has already managed to misplace the Jordan contract and your so lovely files are a disaster."

Stacey laughed obligingly, and told him where he could find an extra copy of the missing contract.

"When are you coming home, *chérie*?" he asked then, and Stacey felt a lump form in her throat at the warm re-gard in his tone. She fought it down before answering. She was through crying, wasn't she?

"I don't know, André. My grandfather's will is rather complicated. Not for a while and maybe…" She paused. There was really no "maybe" about it. She'd already made up her mind and it wouldn't be fair to André not to give him the news now and let him wait two or three months before she finally told him. She took a deep breath. "André, I'm sorry, I don't know how else to say this. But I won't be coming back. I—"

"Not coming back! But why not? We need you here and you are . . . you are like family to us. To me, *chérie*." His Saudi accent had gotten thicker, distorting his French as it always did when he was upset or excited. "Why are you not coming home?"

"Oh, André, thank you for those words! You don't know how I needed to hear *someone* say that I was family now. It's been . . ." Suddenly she found herself telling him all about the details of Henry's will, about the scene in the den after the funeral, about the cancer. About everything, in fact, except what had happened upstairs in the silent, darkened bedroom between her and Ben.

"And you are going to marry this uncle of yours, this Ben?" he asked, very obviously disapproving.

"No, of course I'm not going to marry him, André. But I *am* going to fight him for my half of the ranch."

"And you are never coming back to Paris? Ever?"

Would she go back to Paris? When she had fought Ben and won, when the ranch was half hers, would she want to live here? With Ben? Even if they weren't married?

Yes, she thought, surprising herself. Iron Oakes was her home. "My home is here, André," she said quietly, but forcefully.

And it was, she thought, lying there in her rumpled bed the next morning. Despite everything, the Iron Oakes Ranch was *home* and it was where she was happiest. She couldn't analyze it or explain it, even to herself. It just was. She decided she was going to accept it that way, accept that here in this girlish room with its massive old-fashioned Spanish furniture and its sunshine yellow walls she was far happier than she had ever been in her ultraelegant, ultrafashionable Paris apartment.

She heard the screen door to the kitchen slam as she lay there, heard the click of booted feet over the brick courtyard, then Uncle Pete's Texas twang and the softer, more melodious voice of a man whose mother tongue was Spanish. There was a shout from somewhere beyond the courtyard, muffled by distance, and the booted feet moved away—out toward the barns, she supposed—still talking as they went.

In the silence left behind Stacey heard the unmistakable slap-slap-slap of Marta's hands as they shaped homemade tortillas. The sound evoked a hundred happy childhood memories and served to further strengthen Stacey's resolve and the decision made last night, alone in the aftermath of destructive passion.

Come hell or high water—or Ben—she was here and she was staying!

"But first," she told herself, swinging her long legs out of bed, "first I see that lawyer."

She padded barefoot across the uncarpeted hardwood floor to a small bathroom. It had been a closet at one time; her grandfather had had it converted when she was twelve because, he'd said, a growing girl needed her privacy.

He'd allowed her to pick the colors, and so the tiny room was awash with bright blue tiles running halfway up the walls and a flower-patterned wallpaper in which the predominant color was buttercup yellow. Nothing had been changed, up to and including the flower decals on the mirror and the pink-and-purple paisley bathrobe hanging on a hook behind the door.

"What awful taste I had!" she said aloud as she reached for the gaudy robe.

She shrugged her damp body into it, grimacing at her reflection in the bathroom mirror, and thought longingly of the perfectly plain, perfectly tailored, pearl-colored robe of the finest cashmere hanging on its padded, scented hanger in the walk-in closet of her Paris apartment. Some things, she decided, with a grin at her mirrored self in the too-bright, too-tight robe, would have to be shipped over immediately.

The grin faded as suddenly as it had appeared as she noticed a dark smudge low on her neck. She tugged aside the neckline of the robe to see it better. It was a bruise, a small one, hardly bigger than a dime, just above the curve where her neck and shoulder met. And there was another, fainter one, lower down on the inner curve of her breast. They were, unmistakably, marks made by a man in the throes of passion.

Damn him, she thought furiously, forgetting that she had undoubtedly inflicted the same sort of damage on him. They'd both been overeager and wildly uninhibited last night.

She stared at the faint bruises for a long moment, transfixed by the marks of Ben's possession, and then angrily yanked the robe tight about her. But she could still see the one on her neck where it peeked annoyingly, tauntingly out from the flat collar of the robe, seeming to mock her and remind her of how foolish she'd been.

Quickly she finished her morning ablutions, efficiently plaiting her still-damp hair into a French braid. She applied more makeup than was usual for her, using concealing cream and blusher in an attempt to hide the circles under her eyes and the faint love bite—no, she corrected herself, passion bite—on her neck. A few quick strokes of mascara and a slick of clear gloss and then she returned to the bedroom to stand in uncharacteristic indecision in front of the wide-opened doors of the huge armoire that had become her closet when the bathroom was put in.

The root of her indecision lay in the clothes that hung there. The fashionable, up-to-the-minute wardrobe packed for a long business-related weekend at a French country home was in no way appropriate to life on a working ranch in West Texas. Side by side hung the peach silk lounging pajamas that she had been wearing when the fateful telegram found her, the two black cocktail dresses that Marta had tried and found wanting, the beige suit that she had traveled in and the now infamous dark green Chanel-inspired dress and jacket. Add to that a few pairs of designer slacks and slim skirts in subdued shades of beige, ivory and deep forest green, several tailored silk blouses in coordinating colors and all the appropriate accessories and she still came up zero.

She reached finally for the plainest of the pants, a beige gabardine, front-pleated trouser, and an exactly matching, man-tailored silk blouse. Tossing them across the bed she opened a dresser drawer, looking for the underclothes that Marta had unpacked for her yesterday. What she found brought a gasp of surprise and pleasure to her lips.

Like the robe left hanging on the bathroom door, here too, were her old clothes, neatly folded away with sachets of lavender and rose lovingly tucked between the folds to keep them fresh. Cotton Western-cut shirts and sweaters in the glaringly bright primary colors worn by the old Stacey and soft faded blue jeans, as fashionable now as they had ever been.

"Bless you, Marta," she said aloud as she picked up a pair of the jeans.

Hastily shaking out the folds, she held them up against her. She hadn't grown any taller in the past eleven years and her hips probably weren't much wider, if any. Tossing the garment behind her to the bed, she went back to searching for her underthings. Finally finding what she was looking for, she stepped into a pair of blush pink bikini panties and a matching bra with a flower embroidered in the center of the nearly transparent cups.

She wriggled into the jeans. They were still as tight as ever but, thankfully, she thought, not too tight. She tried on one of her old cotton cowboy shirts but the pearl snaps wouldn't meet over her chest, so she slipped instead into the beige silk blouse, tucking it snugly into her jeans, and automatically fastened a pair of small gold hoops in her pierced ears. A further search didn't turn up any of her old boots, and since her snakeskin pumps would look more than a little ridiculous with the jeans, she stood barefoot in front of the mirror, surveying her finished self.

A snug fit, she decided, twisting around to look over her shoulder at the rear view, but not bad for eleven years. Not bad at all. She turned up the collar of her blouse to further conceal the faint bruise on her neck and then, with a Gallic shrug, nodded to her reflection as if to say, *You'll do*.

Pulling the door closed behind her, she hurried from her room and down the broad staircase, her bare feet making no sound as she crossed the tiled foyer to the den. She made a quick phone call, finding Lyle Higgins most anxious to be of help when she mentioned André's name. They made an appointment for two days hence and she thanked him and hung up. Her next call was to an airline to make reservations on one of the daily flights from Lubbock to Dallas's Love Field. That done, she strolled back through the front hall toward the kitchen and the steady, inviting sound of Marta making homemade tortillas.

"Good morning, Marta," she said, entering through the wide double doors. She didn't bother to look around to assure herself that Ben wasn't there. In the past, he'd always left the house before dawn, and she knew, somehow, that the habit still held.

"Ah, *buenos dias, niña*," said Marta, her hands not pausing in their task. "You slept well, *si*? And now you would like some breakfast?"

"No, no breakfast, thank you, Marta." She headed for the stove where a pot simmered, its rich aroma filling the air. "Just coffee."

But she found herself sitting at one end of the long trestle table, a cup of coffee in front of her, while Marta happily busied herself slicing bread and setting out homemade peach preserves and fresh yellow butter in colorful crockery bowls.

"Benito," she began hesitantly, placing the plate of toast on the table in front of Stacey, "he has told me that you know of Señor Henry's illness."

Stacey didn't look up. "Yes," she said softly, staring into her coffee cup, "he told me about it last night when he came in from the stables. It was something of a shock." Her eyes sought Marta's. "You never wrote me about it, Marta," she said, trying not to sound accusing.

"No, I did not," the housekeeper admitted sadly. "To my shame, I did not. But Señor Henry, he did not want you to know."

"But I had a right," Stacey insisted. "He was my grandfather and I had a right to come back and—oh, I don't know—" she flung a hand out distractedly. "But I could have done something. Anything." She paused.

Railing at Marta wouldn't do any good. What was done was done and she knew Marta hadn't kept it from her willingly, anyway.

"*Sì*, you should have been told," Marta agreed. Her hand went to Stacey's hair, smoothing it back as if she were a child. "Such a proud man, he was, your grandfather," she sighed. "He did not want you to see him as he had become, *niña*, but to remember him as he had been. Big and strong." She cupped Stacey's chin, turning her face up to her own. "Can you understand that, my *niña*, and forgive him?"

Stacey flung her arms around Marta's ample form, hugging her tight. "Yes, I understand, Marta," she said and found that she meant it. Henry *had* been a proud man and she understood pride very well. Too well. "I understand. Thank you."

"Ah, pah!" Marta disengaged herself from Stacey's embrace, embarrassed as always by any display of affection for herself. "Eat your toast before it gets cold," she said gruffly, turning back toward her stove.

Stacey grinned and ate a piece of toast, liberally spread with the peach preserves to please Marta. She was toying with a second piece when the screen door opened and Ben walked into the room.

Immediately, it seemed to Stacey as if the large kitchen had suddenly shrunk. No one said a word, not even Marta, as Ben stood just inside the doorway, his eyes adjusting to the dimmer light of the indoors. And then he moved, breaking the spell as his booted feet clicked noisily against the kitchen tiles. He pulled out one of the ladderback chairs. "Any coffee left?" he asked Marta as he turned it backward and straddled it, facing Stacey as he sat down. He tossed his hat on the table and combed his fingers through his disordered hair. His blue eyes raked over Stacey speculatively, assessingly.

She lowered her eyes, unable or unwilling to face him, as one hand stole nervously upward to pull the collar of her shirt more closely around her throat.

"*Sì*," Marta said in answer to his question, moving to get it for him. She brought the mug to the table but didn't set it down. "You have not taken off your boots," she accused him. "I have just this morning cleaned this floor and now you are tracking it up with dirt!"

He glanced down at the offending boots. "Gee, I'm sorry, Marta." He grinned at her, his strong white teeth looking even whiter against his deep tan. "I forgot."

"Ah, pah! You forgot!" She scolded him fondly, setting the steaming mug down on the table. "You always forget," she continued, lapsing into Spanish.

"I know I do, Marta. I'm sorry." He crossed his forearms on the chair back and leaned forward, gazing up at the housekeeper through his ridiculously long lashes. "Forgive me?" he asked.

Marta threw her plump arms up in a theatrical I-give-up gesture and turned away in pretended annoyance, but she was smiling. When Ben reached out a long arm and tweaked the bow of her apron, untying it, the smile turned to a beam of motherly affection. "Stop that, Benito! You are worse than a baby!" she scolded, slapping his hands and trying to look severe, but failing totally. "Ah, pah!" she said and turned to busy herself at her refuge, the stove.

Stacey watched this foolish play from under her lowered lashes, pretending a great interest in the unwanted toast on her plate. This was a Ben she'd never seen before, she marveled silently. A laughing Ben, showing his affection for Marta with his light-hearted teasing. She wondered when he and Marta had grown so close. Or if they always had been and she'd just never noticed it before because, like most teenagers, she'd always been so wrapped up with how *she* felt.

"Didn't you sleep well?" Ben asked suddenly, breaking into her reverie.

Stacey looked up, startled, realizing belatedly that he was addressing her and not Marta.

"You look a little worn," he elaborated. His eyes touched her face as if seeing under the makeup to the dark circles and then slowly, lingeringly, grazed her throat as if he could see, too, the mark on her neck, even covered as it was by concealer and the collar of her shirt. He smiled.

A slow, knowing smile, thought Stacey. How she'd love to wipe that smirk off his too handsome face! She straightened under his steady gaze, lifting her now-cold coffee to her lips as if she had no idea of what he was referring to, or if she did, that she couldn't care less. "I slept fine, thank you," she said primly, freezing him.

But he wouldn't be so easily frozen. "That's good," he said approvingly, for Marta's benefit she thought, because the housekeeper was listening avidly to their conversation, but his blue eyes still mocked her. Challenged her. "You're ready to go riding, then." The words slipped out before he could stop them; he hadn't meant to invite her to go riding with him. Had he?

"Riding?" She put her cup back on the table but kept her fingers curled around it. She hadn't been for a good, galloping ride in years. She'd love to go riding. But not with Ben. "Not right now, thanks," she said, casting around in her mind for an excuse. If they'd been alone she wouldn't have needed an excuse. She would just say no, but Marta was listening. "I haven't finished my breakfast."

He reached out for the slice of toast on her plate. "I'll help you." He bit into it, making Stacey feel as if it were her he was biting. "You didn't want it, anyway," he added when she started to protest. "Did you?"

"I haven't got any boots," she said then, sticking one bare foot out from under the table. "I found these old jeans in a dresser, but—"

"I thought I recognized the fit," Ben interrupted, his eyes running appreciatively up the length of the slender leg she held out.

Stacey hurriedly pulled it back under the table. Damn! She wouldn't allow him to rattle her again. She would not!

"I have kept your old boots, too, *niña*," Marta was saying. "They are out in the laundry room." She looked pointedly at Ben. "Where yours should be, Benito."

Ben grinned at her. "I'll try to remember that," he said before turning to Stacey. "Any more excuses?" he asked her, wondering why he was pushing. The last thing he wanted was to be alone with her again, except . . .

Stacey looked up into the challenge of his blue eyes and glared at him.

That's why he pushed, he thought. Just to see her flare up that way.

"Why should I go riding with you?" Her tone made a curse of the last word.

Ben shrugged, his shoulders straining against the faded blue of his Western-cut shirt. "I thought you might like to look over the changes in your inheritance," he taunted. "But if you don't want to—" he rose, setting his empty coffee cup on the table "—it's no skin off my nose." He picked up his hat and turned toward the door. "Thanks for the coffee, Marta." He paused. "By the way, there'll be six for dinner tonight. Will that cause you any trouble?"

"Ah, pah! Six is no more trouble than three." She smiled at him and waved him away. "But you must get out of my kitchen so I can work."

Ben grinned and pushed open the screen door, letting it bang after him without another word to Stacey.

She jumped up, nearly toppling her chair. "Wait!" she called and hurried out after him.

The sun-heated bricks of the courtyard were burning hot on her bare feet and she raced past him, hurrying to reach the shaded coolness of the laundry room. Before she could get there, though, she felt herself hoisted into the air from behind, lifted and turned against Ben's broad chest. Automatically, her arms came up to clutch his neck.

He stood still, staring into her face. She stared back, mesmerized by the intense blueness of his eyes. She was so close that she could see the laugh lines crinkling their corners and a small scar, from a run-in with a barbed wire fence if she remembered correctly, just under his left eyebrow. It made him seem vulnerable somehow and strangely sensitive. How odd. Sensitive and vulnerable were two traits that she'd never attributed to Ben before. Seeing them now made her feel uncomfortable and . . . guilty. She squirmed.

His arms tightened of their own volition, stilling her. What was she staring at so intently? What did she see with those cool blue eyes of hers? And why, dammit, did she frown and look away as if she didn't like what she saw?

Her gaze came back to his before he could ask. "Ben," she said hesitantly, questioningly.

"I remember when it took more than a few hot bricks to make you run for your boots," he murmured. His eyes held hers captive as he spoke. His hard male lips were mere inches from her own. She could feel his pulse beating, slowly, steadily, under her hand on his neck. "You've turned into a greenhorn tenderfoot." The words were a caress, as if he'd called her darling.

He's going to kiss me, she thought. And, oh, Lord, how she wanted him too!

"Put me down," she said, panicked at the thought. If he kissed her she'd be lost. She pushed against his chest. "Put me down, Ben," she ordered.

He nodded and set her on her feet. She seemed to hit the ground running toward the laundry room, but it wasn't the heat of the bricks that propelled her—she hardly felt that now. It was the heat in his eyes. She could feel them burning into her back as she ran across the courtyard.

Quickly, she grabbed the first familiar pair of boots she saw, stomping into them barefoot, though she knew she'd pay for that folly later, and hurried out into the sunlight again. She didn't want him to follow her inside. The laundry room was too small and dark and close. She didn't want him that close.

But Ben wasn't coming toward the laundry room. He didn't want to be that close, either. The hell he didn't, he thought savagely, turning in the direction of the high wrought-iron gates that led outside the courtyard. He wanted to be that close and closer. So close that he was inside her again. He pushed open the gate and headed out toward the barn without another word.

Stacey stood for a minute staring after him, watching his long, muscular legs carry him swiftly away from her. And then she broke into a half run after him. Just as she had when she was a little girl, she thought wryly, with a bitter twist to her soft mouth. Ben forging ahead and herself trailing hopefully along behind. Until she'd turned fifteen, and then she'd done the running. But he hadn't chased her.

The barn was only a hundred yards or so beyond the house, about the length of a football field, but it was hot and Ben's stride was long, causing Stacey to take two quick steps to his one. By the time they reached the barn door Stacey's silk shirt was sticking damply to her back between her shoulder blades. She could feel tiny beads of perspiration on her upper lip and at her temples and nape, causing escaping tendrils of hair to curl and cling damply to her moist skin. She surreptitiously daubed her face with the sleeve of her shirt as they entered the shadowed coolness of the barn and almost bumped into Ben as he halted just inside the doorway.

"Riley," he called into the shade-dark barn. "You still here?"

"Yeah, boss, over here," came the muffled reply. A bright, carrot-red head appeared from around the corner of one of the large box stalls, attached to a rakish, freckled face that looked too young for the lean, whipcord body that followed it. He pulled the bottom half of the door closed behind him. "Just checkin' on Lone Star and her new youngun," he said to Ben as his lanky strides ate up the distance between them. "She's got herself the purtiest little filly I ever did—" He broke off, noticing Stacey where she stood just inside the barn door. Her slim figure and pale, golden blond hair was haloed and highlighted by the bright sunlight outside. "Well, maybe not the purtiest," he amended. "You're a mighty purty filly, too," he said to her with a vastly exaggerated twang. "Mighty purty."

"This is Stacey Richards, Henry's granddaughter," Ben said dryly, taking her arm to pull her farther into the barn and out of the revealing sunlight. "*Ms* Richards to you, Romeo. Riley Duggin," he said to Stacey. "Our vet."

The redhead grinned and held out a big, rawboned hand. "Howdy, Miz Richards, ma'am." He winked at her, still exaggerating his drawl. "Real pleased to make your acquaintance, ma'am. 'Deed I am."

Stacey pulled her arm out of Ben's grasp to shake the offered hand and grinned back, charmed by his forthright flirtatiousness. Nobody could flirt like a Texas cowboy—blatantly, playfully, with nothing sly about it. "Please call me Stacey."

Riley stood, his hand still holding hers, gazing with open admiration into her face.

"Uh, could I have my hand please?" she said with a laugh.

"Yes, give the lady her hand back, Riley," Ben said curtly.

Riley dropped her hand like a hot brick and backed away from Ben's frown. "Yes, sir, boss," he said, winking at Stacey. "Yes, sir, don't want to do no rustlin'. No, sir."

Ben snorted with disgust and headed for the stall that Riley had come out of.

Stacey chuckled.

Riley grinned and winked again.

Ben glanced over his shoulder, glaring at them as if they were two kids who were passing notes behind the teacher's back. "You coming?" he demanded peevishly, feeling unaccountably like a fool.

Stacey's chuckle ended in a startled gasp. *If I didn't know better, I'd think he was jealous*, she thought, automatically following them toward the stall.

But she did know better.

What Ben was displaying was pure out-and-out possessiveness, as if she were a . . . a horse or an oil well that he owned, just like any other of Iron Oakes's vast holdings. He obviously thought he'd staked his claim last night, despite the fight they'd had and what she'd said to the contrary. Well, she thought, stomping along behind him, he had another think coming. He could be as possessive as he wanted and it wouldn't do him one damned bit of good.

"How're they doing this morning?" Ben asked the young vet as he opened the bottom door of the box stall.

"Just fine, boss," Riley said, following the bigger man inside.

Stacey paused in the doorway. "Oh, how lovely!" Inside the stall, nursing greedily, was a downy-coated little filly, not yet a full day old. Her long spindly legs were splayed for balance. Her bottle brush of a tail was twitching like a metronome gone haywire.

"She's a beauty," agreed Ben fondly, reaching out to stroke the fuzzy black coat of the baby. The mare nickered and he lifted his hand to her side. "Good girl," he crooned to the proud mother. "You did a real fine job." He circled the mare, smoothing a knowledgeable palm over her satiny coat as he moved around her, checking her over for any signs that she wasn't recovering as quickly as she should from the birth. "The filly's sire is Black Gold," he said, glancing at Stacey over the animal's back.

She looked up at him blankly. There had never been any but cow ponies and rodeo stock eleven years ago. She had no idea what animal Ben was referring to.

"Black Gold," Riley explained before Ben could do it, "Carl Peabody's champion stud. Over Austin way?" he added, as if that would clear it up for her. "He won every race he was in until he injured himself. Includin' the Preakness." He patted the newborn affectionately. "This little lady is gonna be a champion racehorse."

Stacey reached out to stroke the nursing baby. "How can you tell so soon?"

"Bloodlines," Riley said, somehow managing to cover Stacey's hand with his own. "With Lone Star for her mamma and Black Gold for a pappy—" he squeezed her fingers lightly "—why, she wouldn't dare be anything but a champion, now would she?"

Stacey smiled and drew her hand out from under the veterinarian's without making an issue of it. But he got the point, nonetheless. "Maybe she'll turn out to have four left feet," she joked.

Riley widened his eyes as if scandalized. He tucked his fingers into the back pockets of his jeans and rocked back on his heels. "Now she wouldn't da—"

"If you want to take that ride, we'd better get going." Ben bit the words out from between clenched teeth. "Saddle up FlapJack for Miss Richards, would you, Riley?" His voice was perfectly polite, but the words were definitely an order.

Riley looked startled for just a moment. "Sure thing, boss," he said, backing away as Ben came around the mare and exited the stall.

It occurred to Stacey that saddling horses wasn't part of a vet's usual job description, but she said nothing. Ben brushed by her without a glance, and she stood her ground. *What on earth . . . ?* she wondered, lifting puzzled eyes to Riley's.

Riley shrugged. "Ain't nothin' like the green-eyed monster for makin' a rational man plumb unreasonable," he said, grinning at her.

Stacey shook her head. "He's not jeal—"

"You want to take that ride or not?" Ben hollered, his voice cutting across hers.

Riley jerked his head in the direction of the bellow. "Not jealous, huh?" He shrugged. "You sure coulda fooled me."

Stacey stared at the vet, her eyes widening in speculation. Ben jealous? It was an intriguing thought, true, but one she'd already decided was way off base. Jealousy and possessiveness were two entirely different things.

"Stacey, dammit, are you coming?" The voice outside the enclosed box stall held a decidedly testy note.

"You better go before he comes in here an' takes a horsewhip to me," Riley advised her, his grin even wider.

Stacey felt an answering grin turning up her own lips. Why, she wasn't quite sure.

"Stacey!"

With a last quick smile at Riley, she whirled from the stall and ran to catch up with Ben.

7

THEY RODE IN UNEASY SILENCE for a good twenty minutes, Stacey mounted on the buckskin gelding called FlapJack, Ben on a big chestnut with the deep chest and narrowed nose of an Arabian and the powerful, stocky legs of a mustang cow pony.

The day was still, with nothing but the creaking of saddle leather and the muffled clip-clop of the horses' shod hoofs on the dry, hard-packed ground to fill the silence between them. The sun was fierce, beating down on Stacey's bare head as they rode. Sweat trickled between her shoulder blades, and her inner thighs were already beginning to feel the effects of being too long out of a saddle. But all that she could handle, even enjoy. It was the sliding, sideways glances of Ben's that finally began to grate on her nerves.

She shifted her weight in the saddle, wondering what he was plotting now. Judging by the scowl on his face it boded ill for someone. *Probably me*, she thought sourly. In which case, she decided, she didn't really care to hear anything he might have to say. Still, it was going to be an awfully long ride if neither of them said a word.

"I won't have you flirting with the hands," he said abruptly, startling her.

Stacey turned her head to look at him. "You what?" It wasn't that she hadn't heard him, it was just that she couldn't believe what she'd heard.

"You heard what I said." He turned in his saddle to face her. "I won't have you flirting with the hands," he repeated. "Not this time."

"Not this time?" she echoed. Her expression went from puzzled to incredulous to indignant in an instant. She drew herself up in the saddle, poised to do battle. "I haven't been flirting with any of your precious hands," she said coolly, tamping down the anger that his words induced. She wasn't going to lose her temper this time, she vowed silently. Not when he was so obviously trying to make her do just that. "In the first place, I haven't met any to flirt with," she said, the very voice of reason. "And in the second, I—" she paused as a thought suddenly occurred to her.

"Ain't nothin' like the green-eyed monster for makin' a rational man plumb unreasonable."

"You don't—" a genuinely amused smile curved her lips "—you don't mean Riley, do you?" she asked.

Ben glared at her, unamused.

Stacey's smile widened. "Well, I'll be be damned! You *do* mean Riley. I don't believe it. The *jefe* of Iron Oakes is jealous of a freckled-faced, wet-behind-the-ears veterinarian."

"Jealousy has nothing to do with it." Ben redirected his eyes forward, glaring at his horse's bobbing head, trying to ignore her gibe and his own growing sense of foolishness. He could feel the tips of his ears turning red. "I just don't want you giving everybody any more cause for talk, that's all."

Stacey's amused smile faded. "Cause for talk?" she said, but she knew what he meant. Their neighbors were already talking about her long absence and her abrupt return and the supposed reason for it. The last thing she wanted to do was add more fuel to the fire, of course, and if Ben thought—

"I want it to stop," he ordered. "Now, before it even gets started. Is that clear?"

Stacey reined in her horse. "*You* want it to stop?" she said, coolness giving way to irritation at his high-handedness. Although she might have agreed with a reasonable request, she objected—strongly—to an order. "And just who asked your opinion?" she demanded, sitting very straight in the saddle. "Who I flirt with, if I flirt with anyone, is none of your business. Which is completely beside the point in this case," she informed him, "because I wasn't flirting with Riley. I said hello. We shook hands. Tell me—" her voice dripped with delicate sarcasm, making her faint French accent more pronounced "—when did this alleged flirtation take place?"

"It started when you got dressed this morning," Ben said levelly, turning to face her again. "When you put on that flimsy blouse that clings so—" he waved a hand in the air "—so graphically to every curve. And when you piled on the makeup like some Las Vegas showgirl."

"Las Vegas showgirl!"

"And those jeans," Ben went on, ignoring her outburst. "You couldn't get them any tighter if you painted them on. They're a blatant invitation to any man who looks at you."

"Invitation to—?" Stacey sputtered. Unconsciously, her hands tightened on the reins, making her horse snort and shake his head.

"Looking like a common streetwalker may be all the rage in Paris," he said, pinning her to the saddle with the fierceness of his gaze. He was being ridiculous, he knew, and insulting, too, but he couldn't seem to stop himself.

"You might remember that here in Texas we like our women to dress like ladies."

Stacey's hands clenched into fists on her reins. "Just who the hell do you think you are, Ben Oakes?" she demanded. "An authority on fashion as well as—" The buckskin pranced sideways, made increasingly uneasy by the anger communicated to him through his rider's hold. Stacey reined him in tighter, twisting in the saddle to keep Ben in her line of vision as the horse turned. "How can you say such an insulting thing?" Her eyes narrowed dangerously, shooting sparks. "How *dare* you say such a thing!" she spat out, too angry to care that she was being overly dramatic.

Knowing it would infuriate her even further—wanting to infuriate her—Ben shrugged. "I dare because I'm the *jefe* of Iron Oakes now. I dare because you're living in my house. On my ranch," he added, instinctively knowing the exact thing to say to send her over the edge. "And for as long as you're here, you'll live by my rules. Is that clear?"

"*Your* house!" The horse continued to dance uneasily, but Stacey barely noticed it. "*Your* ranch!"

Ben reached out a gloved hand and caught the bridle of her restive mount. "Yes, *my* ranch. And whether you marry me or not, it'll still be my ranch. Remember that."

Stacey stared at him for a long second, trying desperately to contain the feelings that were boiling up inside her. But they were impossible to control, to contain. Eleven years of hard-won self-control snapped like a tightly strung strand of barbed wire. She uttered a sharp scream of pure, unadulterated rage and launched herself at his head.

Ben was completely unprepared for her attack. A grunt of surprise escaped him as her full, furious weight landed square in his lap. He tried to brace himself in the stirrups and one arm came up, automatically circling her back to keep her from falling. His horse, frightened by the sudden additional weight and the screaming, raging wildcat on his back began to prance wildly, bucking slightly in an effort to rid himself of the unaccustomed burden. Ben tightened his gloved hand on the reins, trying to control the panicked animal. His other hand tightened around Stacey's back, trying to control her.

"*Your* ranch!" she screamed, her clenched fists beating wildly at his head and shoulders in an effort to inflict real and permanent damage. She inadvertently knocked his hat off, sending it flying. "It's not your ranch, do you hear me!" One hand caught in his hair. She curled her fingers and pulled. She saw him wince and yanked again, harder, relishing his yelp of pain. "It will never be your ranch!"

"Stacey, calm down!" He could feel her slipping from his one-armed grasp as the chestnut pranced and shifted under them. "You're going to fall."

His only answer was a two-handed yank on his hair and a knee in his thigh as she scrambled for a better position.

"Dammit, Stacey!" He dropped the reins and reached for her wrists with both hands. The horse reared, toppling them backward. Ben twisted his body, taking Stacey's full weight as they fell. Still holding her tightly, he rolled them away from the dangerous, dancing hoofs of the frightened animal.

Stacey scarcely seemed to notice the fall or the barely averted danger of the horse's hoofs. She half raised to her knees, still consumed by the burning need to hurt Ben in any way she could.

He lay passively for a moment, stunned by the fall, his arms crossed protectively over his face, his chest heaving, sucking in great gulps of air to replace the wind that had been knocked out of him. One of Stacey's fists connected with his jaw. With a grunt of pain, he levered himself up and rolled over, trapping her beneath him. Grasping a flailing hand in each of his, he pinned her wrists to the ground on either side of her head, holding her immobile with his weight as he fought to catch his breath.

But Stacey didn't quit. She squirmed wildly, screaming abuse in his ear. Her slim body heaved as she tried to throw him off. Her booted feet kicked uselessly, hitting nothing except her heels on the ground. Enraged anew by his easy ability to hold her down, she retaliated in the only way left to her. She bit him, sinking her teeth into his shoulder with murderous intent.

He reared back pulling his torso out of harm's way. "Dammit, Stacey. That's enough!"

She snarled like a cornered cat and lifted her head again, her teeth bared to take another bite.

He yanked her arms up over her head, manacling her wrists to the ground with one hand, and grabbed her chin in his gloved fingers. "Stop it," he ordered, holding her head immobile. He'd started it, he knew, and he probably deserved to have a strip taken off him, but enough was enough. She was going to hurt herself—or cause him to hurt her—if she kept on this way. "Stop it! Now!" he bellowed into her face.

She stilled, glaring at him defiantly. Her blue eyes were glistening with rage. Her cheeks were flushed with temper and heat and exertion. She was breathing hard, almost panting, and her lips were parted slightly, showing her small, even teeth.

"Same old Stacey," he said with a curious sense of satisfaction. Was this why he'd goaded her so unmercifully? To see how much of the old Stacey was left under the polished veneer of the new?

"Same old Ben," she hissed, trying to twist her chin out of his iron grasp.

He let her, his gaze shifting lower, taking in the madly beating pulse in her slender white throat and, still lower, to her heaving breasts, their every curve revealed by the damply clinging silk shirt. A couple of buttons were missing on the shirt, torn off in her wild struggles, revealing the edges of her pale pink bra and the soft swell of her creamy flesh.

"At least you wear a bra now," he said, his eyes drinking in her exposed cleavage as if mesmerized. He'd tasted her there last night, touched his tongue to that very spot. Without thinking, he bent his head as if to taste her again.

Stacey dug one booted heel into the ground beneath her and arched violently, trying to throw him off. But it was useless; all she succeeded in doing was to further expose her body to his avid gaze.

"Temper, temper," he chided softly, lifting his head to look up into her face. A sudden frown creased his forehead and his gaze traveled back down, his hard fingers sliding down the slim column of her throat to settle on the small, faint bruise on her neck. Worn leather separated his skin from hers. Without taking his eyes off of the bruise, he lifted his hand to his mouth, pulled the glove off with his teeth, and tossed it aside. Then, very gently, he placed his thumb on the mark as if testing for size or shape.

Stacey lay stiffly under him, panting with exertion and temper, sternly forbidding her traitorous body to melt at the sudden, unexpected gentleness of his callused touch and the concern in his eyes. "Don't," she said through clenched teeth. Her eyes shot sparks of helpless fury at the top of his bent head. "Don't touch me."

Ben ignored her protest. He moved his hand to her breast with slow deliberation, nudging aside the silk shirt to fully expose the other faint purple mark. Then he looked up at her, his eyes filled with guilt—and a curiously possessive, almost triumphant light.

"Did I do this?" he asked softly. His index finger brushed lightly, back and forth, over the tangible remnant of their shared passion.

"Yes," she spat at him.

"I'm sorry," he said, very low. And he was, in a way. Sorry that he'd hurt her, but not at all sorry that she wore the marks of his possession. "I didn't mean to hurt you."

"But you did, anyway!" she accused, even though he hadn't really hurt her, not last night, anyway. She'd been so far gone in passion herself that she couldn't have said when the marks were made. But she wasn't going to admit that to him. At the moment, she could barely admit it to herself.

Her eyes held his for an endless second as she tried to silently telegraph messages of repugnance and hate, but communicated instead only pain and bewilderment and some other, sweeter emotion that she couldn't name. Ben reacted to it unconsciously, his expression softening as hers did, his touch becoming even more feather-light and caressing. Against her will, Stacey felt her anger draining away from her, as if it were seeping slowly out into the hot, dry earth beneath her back. She struggled not to let it go; it was all she had to protect herself, she thought desperately.

"I'm sorry, honey," Ben said. He bent his head, lightly pressing his lips over the mark on her neck. "I swear, I didn't mean to hurt you." His head moved lower and his hand cupped her breast, lifting it to his lips as he kissed the faint purplish mark that marred her white flesh. "I never meant to hurt you," he murmured against her skin, nuzzling his face against her breasts. "Never."

Something in her loosened. Some emotion that had been sitting painfully, tightly coiled in her chest slowly unfurled, releasing her furious anger and resettled itself in her stomach. The hands that had been curled into claws in his relentless hold uncurled and opened. Her body, stiff and unyielding beneath his, relaxed and became pliant. Her stubborn, rebellious mind pushed all his hateful words and actions and intentions into the background to be thought about some other time when the demands of her too weak body weren't clamoring to be heard.

She couldn't fight him and herself, she thought despairingly. She didn't even want to fight him—not now, not anymore. But she wouldn't make it easy for him, either. If he wanted her, now, like this, then he would have to take her. Literally.

Ben sensed the change in her almost immediately. He lifted his head from the scented valley of her breasts to look questioningly into her face. Her eyes, half closed against the glare of the sun overhead, seemed to signal her surrender. He released her wrists cautiously, as if fearing she might turn on him again. But her hands lay passively where he had held them, thrown above her head, the palms opened and facing upward like delicate, defenseless flowers. Very slowly, he shifted his weight and lifted himself to one elbow, gazing down at her motionless form.

Her once pristine silk blouse was dusty and torn, the missing buttons leaving it open halfway down the front to expose her breasts in their transparent wisp of pink silk. Her fine blond hair had escaped its neat braid and wavy tendrils curled damply along her forehead and temples and snaked across her white neck. Her eyes were fully closed, the long, mascaraed lashes lying against her cheeks like wounded butterflies.

It was unnatural and unnerving for her to be so still, so meek and passive. He didn't like her this way, with all the fight and fire and personality gone out of her. It wasn't what he wanted at all. It wasn't Stacey, not his Stacey, and it frightened him. Angered him. Made him want to do something so she'd sit up and spit at him again. He lifted his hand from her breast and reached up, brushing the damp tendrils of hair away from her face.

She didn't move, either to acknowledge him, or to squirm away from his touch.

Experimentally, he let his fingers trail down her jaw and across her closed lips, and then lower, down the satin length of her throat to her fragile upper chest.

She lay perfectly still.

He brushed his fingertips lightly over the upper slopes of her breasts.

She didn't respond.

Deliberately then, trying to incite a reaction—any reaction—he traced the contours of the dainty silk flower embroidered on her bra.

The rosy nipple surged into prominence even before he touched it, betraying her need of him, but Stacey wouldn't—*couldn't*—allow herself to move or in any way acknowledge his touch.

Desperate now, he unclasped the front closure of her bra, smoothing it back to reveal the gleaming satin of one white breast. He bent his black head, once again touching his lips to the love bite on the inner curve.

Not an eyelash flickered.

He brushed his lips over the slope of her breast to her nipple. Slowly, he circled the distended bud with the tip of his tongue, around and around the sensitive areola, the way his fingertip had traced the flower, pausing now and then to blow softly against her wet, gleaming flesh.

Except for the goose bumps that rose up along her chest and arms, Stacey didn't move a muscle. She just lay there, limp.

Ben moved his hand downward, skimming over the curves of her waist and hips to trail his fingers seductively up her inner thigh.

Though it was killing her, she didn't acknowledge him by so much as a whimper.

Cursing softly to himself, Ben opened his lips over her breast, taking as much of it as he could inside the wet cavern of his mouth. He cupped his palm between her legs at the same time, caressing her through her jeans.

Stacey tensed beneath him. Her lax hands clenched. *I won't respond*, she thought furiously. *I won't give him the satisfaction!* But the feeling that, moments ago, had settled in her stomach coiled tighter, and then tighter still, burning low in her belly. His mouth, sucking so sweetly, so greedily at her breast, urged her to arch into him. His hand, moving in slow circles between her thighs, urged her to surrender completely to the most erotic caress she'd ever experienced. She longed, with all her passionate being to respond to him. But she wouldn't give in to him now. She couldn't! He'd provoked her anger and her rage. She wouldn't allow him to provoke her passion, too.

She willed herself to lie there, tense and still, her eyes squeezed shut, her nails biting into her own palms, calling upon every last slender shred of self-control she possessed to resist him—and herself. It wasn't easy. It was, in fact, the hardest thing she'd ever done. Her whole body was screaming at her to give in.

Yes, it urged, *Yes, let him love you!*

And then, just when she might have snapped, just when she couldn't have stood even another second of his delicious, wickedly seductive torment, he rolled away from her with a low, muffled curse and sprang to his feet.

"All right, Stacey, you win," he said.

She opened her eyes to see him standing over her, one hand outstretched to pull her to her feet.

"Get up."

She sat up a little shakily and took his offered hand, allowing him to haul her to her feet. Without a word, without so much as another glance in his direction, she bent her head and began fastening her bra and blouse. Her hands were shaking.

Ben turned away, ostensibly to look for his hat and the glove he'd thrown aside, unable to stand there and watch her fumble for her buttons without reaching out to help her—or take her in his arms again. He felt like a damn fool. Worse, like a rapist, as if he'd beaten her into submission and had his evil way. No matter that he hadn't had his way, he still felt guilty. He had plenty to feel guilty about, he thought, snatching up the black Stetson that lay on the ground. He beat it against his leg to rid it of some of the dust and jammed it on his head.

He'd accused her of flirting when she hadn't been; he'd taunted her by calling Iron Oakes *his* ranch; he'd handled her crudely and cruelly. And not just today. Last night his handling had left bruises on her soft flesh. Bruises that he'd been macho enough to feel smug about, he thought with disgust, like some teenage Lothario with more hormones than brains!

"Dammit to hell!" he muttered, bending over to pick up his discarded glove. Straightening, he pursed his lips and issued a piercing, two-note whistle.

The chestnut horse, grazing contentedly a short distance away, raised his head at his master's command and obediently trotted over to Ben with the buckskin following closely behind. He reached out and gathered both sets of dangling reins in one hand.

"You ready to go back?" he asked, staring at his horse's head to avoid looking at her. He was afraid of what he'd see in her eyes if he did—accusation, loathing, fear. Whatever it was, it wouldn't be anything he didn't deserve.

"Yes," she said quietly, not looking at him, either, afraid he'd see the desire she couldn't quite hide.

"Mount up, then." He braced his shoulder against the buckskin and cupped his hand for her booted foot, ready to toss her into the saddle as he'd always done. But she was already mounting herself, her left hand grasping the saddle horn, her foot in the stirrup.

She held out her hand. "My reins," she said, still not looking at him.

"Oh, yeah. Sure." He flexed his knees, circling one arm under FlapJack's neck, and brought the two lengths of leather together over the animal's withers. "Here."

She reached to take them, then gasped and drew back.

"Hell, Stacey, I'm not—" he began, thinking she'd drawn back in fear.

"Your face," she said.

He frowned. "My what?"

"Your face. It's—" she lifted her hand toward him then let it drop "—bruised."

He fingered his jaw, moving it experimentally back and forth. A spot about midway between his ear and chin was slightly tender to the touch. A tiny, self-mocking smile curved his lips. His eyes met hers. "I guess that makes us even."

"I guess," she mumbled, looking away again.

He sighed and extended the reins toward her. "Here, Stacey, take them."

She took them with a mumbled thanks.

Ben continued to stand there, his shoulder against the horse, staring up at her. He wanted to say... something. To explain. But explain what? How could he explain anything when he didn't know himself what had made him act the way he had? There was no rational explanation for the way he'd taunted her. Bullied her. Frightened her. But he could apologize, he thought. He owed her that much, at least.

She looked at him then, leaning forward in the saddle to touch his jaw with gentle fingers. "I'm sorry about your face," she murmured, truly appalled at the damage she'd inflicted, and more than a little embarrassed that she'd lost control to the point of actually hitting someone. Even Ben. It didn't fit in with the image she wanted to have of herself. "Really sorry."

Her apology, so sweetly offered, so obviously sincere, made him feel even worse. "Don't be." He covered the back of her hand with his, crushing it to his cheek so briefly that she wasn't completely sure, afterward, that he had actually done it. "I deserved it." He turned away abruptly and mounted his horse. "I have some work to do out at the cattle pens," he said. "Inoculations and branding. Can you find your way back to the house?"

"Yes, of course, I—" she began, but he'd already whirled the big chestnut and headed off across the flat land, away from her. Stacey sighed—a deep, heartfelt, confused, shaky sigh—and lifted a hand to shade her eyes as she watched the cloud of dust that boiled up behind his retreating figure.

"I deserved it," he'd said. But did he mean for what he'd said and done today? Or for last night?

She hoped not. It gave her a sad, strangely empty feeling to think he might be regretting what had happened between them last night in the shadowed darkness of her room because, to her, last night had been…it had been …

Last night was a mistake, she told herself sternly, clamping a lid on the idiotic sentiments that threatened to overcome her. It had been a thoroughly stupid mistake. A foolish and unfortunate incident that had changed nothing, settled nothing. They were still what they'd been before last night happened. Distant relatives. Strangers. Enemies, even. But not lovers. Never lovers, not in the truest, best sense of the word. The knowledge hurt somewhere deep inside of her.

With a hard yank on the reins, she turned FlapJack in the opposite direction from the one Ben had taken and set her heels to the horse's sides, leaning low over his neck as he surged forward. They ran a mile or more, woman and horse, pounding furiously over the hot, dry ground as if the devil himself were after them. Stacey urged her mount faster and faster still, running from herself, from Ben, from all the painful decisions made or still to be made. Running …

The horse stumbled, his hoof grazing some unseen rodent hole, throwing Stacey forward in the saddle so that she had to clutch his mane to keep from falling. Cursing under her breath, she regained her balance and pulled gently on the reins, slowing the horse to a halt. She could feel his sides heaving between her legs. Hot puffs of air billowed from his flared nostrils.

PLAY THE
LUCKY
CARNIVAL WHEEL
scratch-off game
and get as many as
SIX FREE GIFTS . . .

HOW TO PLAY:

1. With a coin, carefully scratch off the silver area at right. Then check your number against the chart below it to find out which gifts you're eligible to receive.

2. You'll receive brand-new Harlequin Temptation® novels and possibly other gifts—ABSOLUTELY FREE! Send back this card and we'll promptly send you the free books and gifts you qualify for!

3. We're betting you'll want more of these heartwarming romances, so unless you tell us otherwise, every month we'll send you 4 more wonderful novels to read and enjoy. Always delivered right to your home. And always at a discount off the cover price!

4. Your satisfaction is guaranteed! You may return any shipment of books and cancel at any time. The Free Books and Gifts remain yours to keep!

NO COST! NO RISK!
NO OBLIGATION TO BUY!

More Good News For Members Only!

When you join the Harlequin Reader Service®, you'll receive 4 heartwarming romance novels each month delivered to your home at the members-only low discount price. You'll also get additional free gifts from time to time as well as our newsletter. It's ''Heart to Heart''—our members' privileged look at upcoming books and profiles of our most popular authors!

If offer card is missing, write to: Harlequin Reader Service, 901 Fuhrmann Blvd., P.O. Box 1867, Buffalo, NY 14269-1867

Immediately contrite at her callous use of the willing animal, she dismounted and ran her hands expertly down his legs, checking for any damage that might have been done by his near fall, cooing soothingly to the horse all the while. His neck and chest were damp with sweat, but thankfully, he was whole.

She remounted and gazed around her to get her bearing, unsure how far or in what direction they'd run. Sighting a familiar landmark, she gathered up the reins and spoke softly to the horse, urging him to a cooling walk. They moved slowly in the direction of the little family cemetery where Henry Oakes had been buried yesterday morning. Swinging out of the saddle, she tied FlapJack to the white wrought-iron fence surrounding the tidy plot—not at all sure that he would respond to her whistle—and pushed open the gate.

It was green in the cemetery, just as it was around the house, thanks to its windmill-generated irrigation system that watered daily, and a few transplanted oaks and red maples. The trees weren't as large as the ones surrounding the house because they'd been planted later, but they still offered shade and the welcome illusion of coolness.

Her parents were buried here. The two simple marble markers that stood side by side were engraved with names and dates that meant little to her. She'd been less than six months old when a fatal auto accident claimed their lives. They were snapshots in a photo album, less real to her than the woman buried beneath the impressive headstone next to her grandfather's grave.

She trailed her hand over the gleaming white marble angel that marked the resting place of Constance O'Flannery Oakes, the beloved and eternally mourned wife of Henry Oakes. She'd died before Stacey was born, before her own daughter was old enough to start school, but there was a painting of her hanging opposite the big brass bed in Henry's bedroom, and Stacey had come to know her through that. Connie Oakes had been a gentle soul, fair and delicate with a sweet smile and under-standing eyes.

"She was the only person could ever calm ol' Henry down when he was a ragin' or turn him aside from some fool scheme," Uncle Pete told her once. "Jes one of her sweet smiles was all it took. An' she would'a done any-thin' fer him. Anythin' a'tall. Couldn't find no finer woman."

Stacey sank to her knees beside her grandfather's grave, reaching out to sift the new-mounded earth through her fingers, wondering if Grandmother Connie would have been able to "turn him aside" from his lat-est—last—fool scheme. Whatever it was.

"Oh, Henry," she whispered. "Why did you do this to me? Why? Your Connie wouldn't have liked it." She cocked her head sideways, looking at the headstone as if Henry Oakes were sitting there in front of her. "I know you had a reason," she rationalized. "You always do— did," she amended, patting the earth as if to soothe. "I just wish you could tell me what it was."

She fell silent, as if she actually expected some kind of answer, but the air was still and quiet except for the oc-casional gentle snorting of FlapJack, tied at the fence, and the rhythmic creaking of the windmill. A hawk soared through the sky above her, a rattler slithered through the prairie grasses just beyond the fence, a lone cow lowed somewhere off in the far distance and still she sat— thinking, remembering, drinking in the peacefulness around her and, finally, making her own peace with the memory of her grandfather.

Theirs had been a stormy relationship those last few years they'd had together. They'd both hurled some hurtful words at each other, leaving unsaid other words that should have been spoken. They were both too stubborn and too proud and too much alike to have done anything else, she realized. But it didn't really matter. Not now. Not anymore. What mattered was the relationship they'd shared for the first fifteen years of her life.

"Goodbye, Henry," she said softly, getting to her feet. She looked down at the simple headstone, adorned with the Iron Oakes brand, and smiled. "I love you. I've always loved you."

8

STACEY STOOD in front of her bedroom mirror trying to adjust an oblong scarf of peach-and-ivory silk around her neck to fall in graceful folds. She'd had a shower when she came in from her ride, and a brief, uneasy nap to rid herself of a nagging sun-and-emotion-induced headache. Her hair was coiled into a smooth French twist at the back of her head. Her makeup was fresh and expertly applied. Her slim body was clothed in peach silk evening pajamas with a loose, dolman-sleeved top and slim, tapered pants that made her legs look elegantly long.

She was herself again, she thought with relief. Cool. Collected. Completely in control.

As long as no one noticed the touch of sunburn on her nose and forehead, she amended, or looked too closely at the palms of her hands, blistered by the leather reins, or the heels of her feet, blistered, too, from wearing her old cowboy boots without socks. They were painful where the straps of her delicate high-heeled sandals rubbed against them. The insides of her thighs ached, too, and her backside from the unaccustomed hours in the saddle today.

Impatiently she untied the scarf and retied it into a big pussycat bow, standing back to study the effect. No, she thought—tied that way it spoiled the sleek lines of her outfit, besides being much too obvious. She looked like a teenager trying to hide a hickey from her parents. She pulled the scarf off altogether, but that was worse. The wide neckline of the top, meant to slide easily off either shoulder, exposed the faint purplish mark on her neck completely.

It looked huge to Stacey, obvious and noticeable, like a brand. It could be nothing other than what it was; a mark inflicted by a man in the throes of passion. She couldn't pass it off, like her torn, dusty blouse as being caused by a fall from her horse.

That had been her excuse when she'd brought Flap-Jack back to the barn—that she'd taken a fall. Riley had looked at her a little strangely but seemed to believe her story.

She draped the scarf around her throat again, letting the ends trail down the back instead of the front. Worn like that, it looked more like an intended part of the out-fit instead of an afterthought. Rummaging through her jewelry case, she fastened on big square earrings of hammered gold and slipped a matching cuff bracelet on her left wrist. Satisfied that she'd done her best, she shrugged at her reflected image and left the room.

Her high heels clicked noisily on the stairs, masking the low murmur of voices coming from the living room, announcing her descent to anyone who might have been listening for it. As she reached the bottom of the stair-case Ben appeared in the arched doorway. Her first cow-ardly impulse was to turn and run back to the safety of her room, but she resisted it. She stood, outwardly poised, on the bottom step. She looked, he thought, as fragile and elegant and as cool as a crystal glass of peach sherbet.

He stood without moving, staring back at her, his black head nearly brushing the curving arch. Instead of his usual denim jeans and workshirt, he wore well-tailored black slacks that fitted snugly over his flat belly and narrow hips and fell to just the right length over a pair of cowboy boots made of exotic blue-sheened eel skin. His white shirt with its pearl snaps and Western-cut yoke emphasized his wide, powerful shoulders and chest. A silver concha buckle decorated his belt. He wore no tie, not even a Western string one, and the collar of his shirt was left open, exposing a small wedge of the dark curling hair on his chest. A small bruise stood out sharply on his clean-shaven jaw.

"You're looking well after your fall," he said. The way he emphasized the last word told her he'd heard her story from Marta or Riley, and was amused. His eyes went significantly to the flowing scarf at her neck and he grinned conspiratorily.

Almost against her will, Stacey found herself grinning back, feeling like a co-conspirator who shared a secret with him, a secret that must be hidden from everyone else. She wondered what story he had told to explain away the small bruise on his jaw. Her grin faded. Suppose he'd said he'd fallen, too?

He moved toward her reaching out to cover her hand where it rested on the newel post.

Stacey snatched her hand back automatically, fearful of what his slightest touch did to her.

Ben's eyes flickered up in surprise and a sort of pain crossed his face, but the expression was gone before Stacey could be sure she'd read it right.

"I won't bite you," he said, and the word "again" hung in the air between them. Unconsciously, he curled his hand around the newel post, pressing his fingers into the wood.

"Is that a promise?" she shot back. But the words, even to her own ears, sounded more like a plea than the sarcastic rejoinder she'd intended them to be.

At her words his eyes went again, deliberately, to the scarf draped across her throat. Her hand stole upward, nervously fingering the length of silk, as if reassuring herself that the mark of his mouth was still hidden.

I've faced down an Arab sheik who once tried to buy me from André, she reminded herself. *I've easily turned off countless playboys of all nationalities with just a polite smile. So why can't I do it with Ben?* She dropped her hand to her side, her back stiffening proudly. *I will not allow him to intimidate me,* she told herself bravely, ignoring the agitated fluttering of her pulse as their eyes met again.

Let him see how icy she could be, she thought. How really cold and unmelting. Maybe that would protect her from the heat in his eyes. But surprisingly, she saw no heat there now, just two eyes as blue and unreadable as the summer sky over Texas gazing back at her. Waiting.

In that instant she felt, somehow, as if he'd defeated her. Bested her in some way she couldn't understand. He could so easily affect her, stirring her to hot rage or hotter passion, but she could stir him only if he chose to let her. And if he didn't choose then . . . nothing.

Damn him! she thought vehemently. And damn her own weak will where he was concerned.

With a toss of her head, she tore her eyes away from his and swept past him, through the archway and into the living room. Ignoring the pain of her shoe straps where they rubbed against her blistered heels, she crossed the room to join the little group by the open patio doors. Three of the group were men—Uncle Pete, the redheaded vet, Riley, and a Mexican *vacquero* of about fifty with a lean, wiry body and weather-beaten skin. The fourth person was a lovely young woman with a cascade of dark curls tumbling to her shoulders and dark liquid eyes. She looked up, smiling as Stacey approached them, and poked Riley in the side with her elbow. He broke off whatever he was saying and held out his hand.

"Good to see you all in one piece after your fall," he said, hardly a trace of twang coloring his voice now as he moved aside to make room for her in their circle. "How're you feeling?"

Stacey glanced up at him, looking for the barb in his words. His eyes still twinkled as irrepressibly as she remembered from this afternoon, but she could see no hidden meaning in them. "Much better, thank you," she said, taking a second, closer look at him. His hair still blazed carroty red, faint freckles still dusted his nose, but he seemed older than what she'd first thought. It was his voice, of course. "What happened to the accent?" she asked, smiling up at him.

He grinned, unabashed at being caught in his little deception, and turned to introduce her. "Stacey Richards, meet Francisco Montoya. Cisco's the Iron Oakes foreman," he told her. "Been here for the past—" he looked at the foreman "—for what? The past five years or so?"

"Six," he said in his musically accented English. He shifted his drink and held out a hand to Stacey. "Good evening, Señorita Richards."

"Call me Stacey, please."

"Stacey," he said obediently, releasing her hand.

"And this is Linda Montoya, Cisco's daughter," Riley said. "She's on summer vacation from college."

The two women shook hands. "What college?" Stacey asked pleasantly.

"SMU. I'm a junior." She smiled at her beaming father and corrected herself. "Going to be a junior next fall."

"SMU's a wonderful school, I've heard," Stacey said. It was where she would have liked to have gone.

"Yes, it is," Linda agreed.

"Heard you got throw'd," Pete said then, adding his two bits to the conversation with characteristic disregard for what was being discussed. "Marta was all wound up about it, but you don't look much hurt to me."

"Just my pride, Uncle Pete," she said and then tried to change the subject. The less said about her "fall," the better. "How's a girl get a drink around here?"

"What would you like?" asked Riley.

"White wine, please." She smiled up at him. "Or red, or rosé." She shrugged delicately, recalling that Iron Oakes had never had much of a wine cellar. "Whatever's open."

He moved away to get it for her and Pete went on as if there hadn't been an interruption. "Never heard of ol' FlapJack throwin' nobody afore," he said. "He's a pure gentle animal."

"He didn't exactly throw me, Uncle Pete," Stacey told him. "It was my fault entirely." She paused to flash a smile of thanks at Riley for her wine and took a small sip before continuing. The white wine was crisp and refreshing. "He stepped in a hole. And I went off over his head."

"Ridin' hellbent for leather, I'll be bound," Pete said gruffly, giving her an approving slap on the back that caused her to choke a little on her wine. "This li'l girl always did know jes one way to ride a horse," he said to no one in particular. "And that was at a dead run. Caused poor ol' Marta no end a grief, she did. One way or t'other." He grinned, pleased. "Never knowed if you was gonna find her with her arm broke or behavin' real un-

ladylike and beatin' up on some poor cowboy who
daren't defend himself. Had a real mean temper, she did."
He chuckled to himself as if something funny had just
occurred to him. "Ol' Ben came in today lookin' like
you'd been beatin' up on him," he informed her.

Stacey gasped and choked on her wine again, tipping
the glass in the process so that Riley reached out to rescue it from her suddenly clumsy fingers. Pete started
pounding her on the back. "Hell's bells, girl, if you cain't
keep it down, don't drink it."

"Sorry," she mumbled, trying to avoid his helping
hand. "I usually handle my liquor better," she laughed
shakily, "but it went down the wrong way. I'm fine,
really."

Riley handed her back her glass. "Okay, now?"

"Fine, thanks," she said, avoiding looking at him as she
took the glass. Riley was no dummy, despite his aw-
shucks-ma'am looks, and she'd gotten the distinct
impression this afternoon that he only half believed her
story, no matter how politely he'd pretended to believe
it. "Did Ben say how he hurt himself?" she asked Pete as
casually as she could manage.

"A little heifer kicked me when I tried to brand her,"
said a mocking voice behind her.

"Objected to your handling, did she?" The words were
out before she could stop them. She knew better than to
needle Ben, especially in front of an audience, but she just
couldn't seem to help it.

"At first," he said, "but then she just bowed to the
inevitable and let it happen. Like they all do," he added
softly. He knew she couldn't respond to that without
giving herself away.

If she hadn't already, she realized belatedly. Uncle Pete
looked faintly puzzled at the biting undercurrents in their

apparently harmless comments and Francisco Montoya wore an uneasy expression as if he, too, sensed something not said. Linda's dark eyes were bright with speculation. Riley's darted back and forth between her face and Ben's.

She didn't know what he saw, if anything, in Ben's face because he still stood behind her and she refused to turn around. If she had, she would have seen that his expression was as carefully bland as her own, giving nothing away and so making Riley even more suspicious.

"Come, everyone. Supper is ready," Marta announced from the arched doorway, diffusing the tension. Everyone turned with visible relief toward the dining room.

The table was again beautifully set, with the addition of candles and cut flowers tonight. Ben steered everyone to their seats as unobtrusively and graciously as André would have done, gallantly seating Marta before taking his own chair at one end of the table. Stacey found herself seated at the opposite end, so that every time she looked up across the expanse of old lace and sparkling crystal she encountered Ben.

He no longer looked at all like the hick cowboy she'd tried to convince herself he was. If the truth were known, he'd stopped being a hick in her mind sometime during the heated encounter of the previous night. But the truth wasn't known, even to her, and she was amazed at how he seemed to be filling her eyes with a hundred different aspects of himself.

He looked as if he belonged sitting there at the head of the gracious table, as at home among these elegant surroundings as he was on the back of his chestnut cow pony. He had an aura of competence and command and power that was somehow right in both places. Not power just by virtue of his size and obvious strength, but on the basis of sheer personality. He dominated the table in a very subtle way. It was to him that everyone turned for agreement or confirmation of a point in dispute. It was for him they told their jokes and their stories. It was his approval and laughter they sought as their reward.

He threw his head back now in rich enjoyment of something Pete said, and Stacey found herself unwillingly fascinated by the play of muscles in his strong, brown throat and the flash of his teeth, sparkling white against the tan of his face and by his hard, masculine lips, parted in laughter. He reached for his wineglass, his big hand looking stronger and more tanned in contrast to the fragile crystal, and brought it to his lips. Stacey felt suddenly as if she were that glass, so fragile and helpless under the onslaught of his hand and lips.

She looked away, replying quite coherently and with apparent interest to a question from Riley. She managed, in fact, to appear interested and interesting to everyone at the table, speaking when she was spoken to, laughing in the right places and contributing much of her own to the general conversation. Her years at finishing school and as André's official hostess had taught her the trick of appearing to be fascinated by conversation she was only half listening to while her mind was busy elsewhere. And tonight, try as she might, her mind was very definitely elsewhere. Not far elsewhere, just to the other end of the table, but she couldn't seem to help herself.

She watched silently with an unacknowledged ache somewhere deep inside her when Ben's black head bent companionably toward Linda, who sat on his left, as he listened earnestly to whatever she was saying. He smiled and reached out to teasingly tweak a dangling tendril of her dark hair. The back of his hand brushed her cheek caressingly. His smile softened his lips as even laughter hadn't done and his face was full of genuine warmth and tenderness as he looked down at the young woman.

The way he used to look at me, remembered Stacey with a pang, *before I grew up and we started hating each other*.

Does he love her? she wondered, looking away when she couldn't bear to watch any longer. He didn't look like a man in love, she thought, but then, who could tell from appearances? Ben had never been one to display his emotions openly. Still, she had to admit that Linda would be perfect for him. She was sweet and charming; she was a Texan to her bones; and she obviously had a giant-size crush on the *jefe* of Iron Oakes. It would be a miracle, really, if the feeling weren't mutual.

Stacey glanced back down the length of the table, unable to keep her eyes away for long. Ben and Linda were still deep in conversation. He seemed to be trying to re-assure her of something, shaking his head and then turning to Marta, who sat on his other side, to back up whatever he'd said.

Marta agreed with an emphatic nod and Ben laughed again, reaching out to pat Linda's hand where it lay on the table. Linda smiled up at him then, apparently re-assured.

Stacey's fingers tightened on her fork as if she intended to break it in half with just her bare hands. She lowered her eyes to her plate, afraid that someone might see the emotion that burned in them.

Jealousy. Oh, the jealousy! It twisted in her stomach as strongly and as painfully as it ever had in her lovesick teens. She realized, miserably and unwillingly, that she hadn't yet grown out of loving Ben. She would probably never grow out of loving him, hating him, wanting him.

She took a deep breath, consciously drawing back from the edge of the overwhelming emotion on which she hovered for only a very few seconds, endless though they'd seemed. She became aware that her nails were pressed painfully into her palm and she looked at her hand, realizing with a shock that she held the fork as if it were a weapon. Carefully she uncurled her fingers and put the utensil down next to her plate, looking around the table to see if anyone had noticed her lapse.

No one had. They were all busy with the business of finishing dinner and selecting their desserts from the mouth watering pantry tray that Marta's helper, Consuela had brought into the dining room.

"Uncle Pete," Stacey said as casually as she could to the man on her right, shaking her head at Consuela to decline the offered desserts. "I need to get to the Lubbock airport tomorrow. Do you think that nice kid—Hank, wasn't it?—would be free to drive me into town?"

"You ain't leavin' already, girl?" Pete said, his gravelly voice carrying down the length of the table. "You jes got here! Ain't nothin' been settled yet an' you ain't made no weddin' plans or . . ." He caught the look in Stacey's eyes and for once in his life was aware of having said something he shouldn't. "Or nuthin'," he finished lamely.

"I have no intention of making any wedding plans," she said. "I'd merely like to go into Dallas for a few days." She shrugged. "Do a little shopping and—" she paused, deliberately seeking Ben's eyes to issue her challenge directly "—see my lawyer about contesting Henry's will."

There, it was said out loud. The gauntlet thrown down. Her intentions made clear. *Now let's see what he does with it*, she thought, feeling unaccountably victorious until she caught sigh of Marta's astonished face. The older woman shook her head slightly, shocked and disapproving. One did not challenge the *jefe* publicly, her look said clearly. Not unless one wanted a public reprisal in return.

But Ben's words, when he answered her challenge, were mild. "I'm going to Dallas myself tomorrow," he said, not even bothering to pick up the gauntlet she'd thrown. Not even seeming to realize, she thought, that one had been cast at his feet. "You can hitch a ride with me."

She shook her head. A drive from the ranch to Dallas was much too long a time to be trapped in a car with only Ben for company. They'd tear each other apart. "I'd rather fly, thanks."

"You will be."

Stacey looked at him blankly.

"We had an airstrip put in a few years ago," he explained. "Just a small one, but it serves the purpose."

"And a helicopter pad," Pete added, his tone of voice indicating disapproval.

"Really?" Stacey was interested in spite of herself. "What for?"

"Herdin' cattle," Pete told her, shooting a look of good-natured disgust at Ben. "College boy here calls it modern ranchin'."

Ben laughed obligingly at what was obviously an often heard refrain and then turned his attention back to Stacey. "Do you think you can manage to be up before ten tomorrow?" he asked her. "I'd like to get an early start."

"I think I can manage that, yes," she said, and turned away as Consuela offered her an after-dinner drink. "Courvoisier, please," she said to the maid. She rose from her chair with the heavy crystal brandy snifter in her hand. "Let's have our coffee and afters on the patio, shall we?" she said to the table at large, moving toward the courtyard with all the grace and assurance of a young queen.

Ben had placed her at one end of the table, she told herself. It was traditionally the place of the hostess. Probably he'd only intended to seat her as far away from him as possible, with no intention of conferring any sort of status on her. But, dammit, she *was* the hostess in this house. It was time she started acting like it.

"Bring the coffee trolley outside, Consuela," she said, avoiding Marta's eye as she moved down the length of the table toward the patio doors. "It's much too lovely a night to waste indoors."

9

STACEY SAT QUIETLY, her long nylon-clad legs crossed at the knee, her hands resting easily on the padded arms of the chair as she waited, with seeming patience, for the lawyer to finish reading her grandfather's will.

She was aware that she created a very cool picture, but the image she presented was misleading because she was anything but calm. She hadn't been calm or cool or really sure of anything since she left Paris. *Couldn't he read any faster?* she asked herself, staring at the lawyer's bent, balding head, willing him to finish. He seemed to sense her eyes on him and looked up quickly, catching her impatience before she could hide it.

"Just a couple more paragraphs," he reassured her with a smile.

Stacey returned his smile and shook her head slightly as if denying her impatience, wanting him, for some reason, not to know how important this was to her. But he had already returned to his perusal of the will.

Silly, she chided herself silently. One is supposed to hide nothing from one's lawyer. André had taught her that. You found a lawyer you could trust, he said, and then you trusted him. Always, of course, paying him very well to ensure that he stayed trustworthy. She smiled, thinking of André.

"May I ask you a question?" the lawyer asked, interrupting her thoughts, and Stacey nodded. "What do you want?"

"What do I want?" she echoed, slightly puzzled. Wasn't it obvious what she wanted?

"You don't like the will as it's written, obviously, or you wouldn't be here. So the next question is what do you want? Am I supposed to look for a way to disinherit Ben Oakes and this—" he looked down briefly "—this Peter Crawley totally, or—"

"Oh, no," Stacey interrupted. "That's not what I want at all! Uncle Pete is . . . was Henry's partner," she explained, "from their earliest wildcatting days. He's not actually my uncle, not by blood, but he's always been at Iron Oakes. Uncle Pete is family. Just like Marta and like Ben," she added honestly because Ben had been, still was, part of her family no matter how she felt about him now.

"I take it, then, that you don't want to disinherit Mr. Oakes, either," he prodded patiently, when her voice trailed off.

"No," she said slowly. "I want Ben to have everything Henry felt was due him. Even half the ranch. That's only fair. He's worked it all these years. But I also want what's due me and I don't want to have to marry Ben to get it."

"That clause applies only to the ranch," Lyle Higgins pointed out, thinking that perhaps she didn't clearly understand the terms of the will. "There are no strings attached to the other bequests."

"I understand that," she assured him.

"And Mr. Oakes has to pay you for what would have been your share of the ranch, so you would lose nothing."

"Yes, I understand that, too," she said, becoming impatient. Did André really think that Lyle Higgins was the best lawyer in Texas? He seemed just a tad slow to her.

"What you don't understand, Mr. Higgins, is that what I *want* is my half of the ranch. Not the money, the ranch."

"Ah," he said. "First question answered. Now for the second. Why?"

"Because it's my home. I grew up there." Her hands fluttered for a moment in front of her as she tried to explain, and as if she had suddenly become aware of them, she clasped them together in her lap. "I want it, that's all," she said finally, quietly. "And I don't want to have to marry Ben to get it." She looked the lawyer straight in the eyes. "Can you help me?"

"That depends, Miss Richards, on several things." He paused, looking vaguely uncomfortable and Stacey wondered what was coming. "If you'll forgive me for asking, how are you and Ben Oakes related? Aside from legally, that is. I mean, is he, ah . . ."

"You mean is Ben Henry's bastard?" she said crudely when he hesitated. "No, he isn't. Not literally, anyway." She reached for her handbag. "Forgive me. Bad joke," she said, rummaging through the purse for her cigarette case. "Damn," she swore under her breath when she couldn't find it.

"Problem, Miss Richards?"

Yes, there was a problem. But not one he could do anything about. It was just that every time the supposed relationship between Ben and herself was mentioned lately she started falling to pieces. He was *not* related to her by blood! Why did everyone need to ask that question?

"I seemed to have misplaced my cigarettes," she said finally, because Lyle Higgins was waiting for an answer to his question.

"Allow me." Mr. Higgins came around his desk and offered her one of his from an enameled box, lighting it for her before he sat down again.

Stacey inhaled deeply, even though she didn't really like American cigarettes, feeling the rush of soothing smoke invade her lungs before she spoke. "When Ben was first adopted," she began reluctantly, "there were rumors. Lots of rumors. Some are still probably floating around but—" she shook her head, causing the gold hoops in her ears to swing gently "—none of them were or are true."

"How can you be sure of that? Was it ever investigated?"

She shrugged. "I don't really know, but its not relevant, anyway." She paused and took a long, slow drag on her cigarette, gathering together her thoughts to tell this man how she knew.

He sat quietly, hands clasped on his desk, waiting for her answer.

"I'm sure because Henry loved Ben," she said after a minute. "Very much. And the feeling is . . . was mutual. They were as devoted as any real father and son. More so, maybe," she continued, reflectively, "for having chosen that relationship. If Henry had even *suspected* that Ben was his biological son, he'd have said so. Hell," she reached over and crushed out the half-smoked cigarette, "he'd have taken out a front-page ad in every newspaper in Texas to announce the fact. And besides that," she went on, unconsciously using almost the same words that Ben had said to her, "if Ben and I were related *that* way, by blood, if there had been any doubt at all in Henry's mind that Ben might really be my uncle, then he'd never have put in the marriage clause. My grandfather was a hard man, Mr. Higgins, and he made up a lot of his own rules as he went along, but he had a strong moral streak. Religious, even. He was raised a Baptist, you know, even though he didn't actively practice, and he would have considered even the possibility of such a thing highly immoral."

"Can it be proved one way or another?"

Stacey shrugged, indicating that she didn't know. "Is it important?"

"It could be our whole case."

He had her full, undivided attention then. "How?"

"Under Texas law, Miss Richards, a marriage between an uncle and niece who are related by whole or half blood is illegal. It carries a two- to ten-year penitentiary sentence, plus, of course, automatic dissolution of the marriage. However, marriage between an uncle and niece related by adoption alone carries no such restrictions."

"Which is my situation exactly, so I don't see how that—" she began but he held up his hand and, when she was silent, continued.

"You don't know, *for sure*—" he emphasized the words "—if that's your situation or not, do you, Miss Richards?" he said slowly. "Your blood relationship to Ben Oakes, or lack of it, has never been proved one way or the other."

"You mean—" Stacey leaned forward in her chair "—I could just say that I *believe* that Ben is my blood uncle and—" light was beginning to dawn "—and the burden of proof would be on him to prove I was wrong. Is that what you're saying."

"Exactly."

"Could I have another cigarette, please?" she said, needing time for what she'd just heard to sink in. She inhaled deeply as he lit it for her. "Thank you," she said absently, leaning back in her chair.

She didn't have to prove anything then, she thought, she had only to insinuate it. No, it couldn't be that easy. Nothing involving Ben was easy.

"What if Ben can prove it?" she asked. "That he's not Henry's biological son, I mean. There must be records of some sort, mustn't there? From a hospital or something. Or Marta," she said, remembering. "Marta Suarez is our housekeeper," she explained. "She's mentioned in the will, too. Ben is Marta's sister's child." She frowned. "I think. At least, that's what I remember being told."

The lawyer shrugged. "If he can prove he's not your grandfather's biological son, then your case would be more difficult, of course, but not impossible. We would merely contend that *you* have always looked upon Mr. Oakes as your uncle, or your older brother, and that any other relationship would be morally abhorrent to you. Not sound legal grounds, I admit, but highly emotional ones. And juries are often swayed by emotion."

The word hit her with the force of a punch to the gut. Juries. She hadn't thought of juries before. She'd been imagining this while thing on paper, like one of André's oil deals. Rather impersonal. But juries?

Her face flamed suddenly, remembering the passion shared in her darkened bedroom, his big callused hands, hot and eager on her body and his mouth—his avid, greedy mouth—as it hungrily caressed hers. Her own as she caressed him. Definitely not actions a woman permits to a man that she thinks of as an uncle.

If she took Ben to court, challenged him with the emotional case that Mr. Higgins suggested, he could tear her apart. But would he? She didn't know. But she did know that she hadn't thought of him as an uncle since she was fourteen. And she knew that he knew it, too. Marta knew it. Even Uncle Pete probably knew it. If they were brought into court, where would their loyalties lie? Would they side with her or with the *jefe* of Iron Oakes?

"No, I don't think so," she said, not realizing that she'd spoken aloud until the lawyer looked at her questioningly. "I don't think I can take it into court, not on those grounds. It sounds so—" her hand fluttered "—so sordid. If there was something else, some other way, maybe. But not on that basis—" she shook her head "—I don't know."

"In most cases I'd agree, Miss Richards. It certainly isn't the most savory way to go about it. But in this instance it might be the best way. Not the only way, mind you, just the best."

"Why?" Stacey asked, her stare intent as she waited for his answer.

"Well, in the first place, any court hearing would be here in Texas. Mr. Oakes's home ground. Yes, I know you were born here," he said quickly, anticipating her, "but you don't live here now. You're a foreigner. You look foreign. You have a foreign accent. Very faint, true, but there.

"Secondly, you yourself have told me that you haven't lived on the ranch for eleven years, not even been back for a visit. You have a job in Paris, an apartment. Also, you've been receiving a very hefty monthly income from your grandfather these past eleven years. He hasn't stinted in his care of you, even though you've shown an apparent lack of proper family feeling.

"I said 'apparent,' Miss Richards," he added when she opened her mouth to speak, "and it is appearances that we must concern ourselves with. Moreover, and most detrimentally, you lose nothing, financially speaking, as the will now stands. Your monthly income will continue." He glanced down at the will. "You will own several Oakes Enterprises oil leases and other subsidiaries outright *and* you will be financially compensated for half of the Iron Oakes Ranch if you decide to sell. In short, Miss Richards, you've been remembered most generously in your grandfather's will and I'm afraid that any attempt to overthrow this one clause, except on the grounds I have already mentioned, is doomed to failure."

"That's what Ben said," Stacey said after a minute. "He said most Texas juries wouldn't take kindly to a woman who hadn't seen her grandfather in eleven years fighting like a greedy bitch to get more," she repeated hollowly, looking down at the cigarette in her hand. "He said they'd most likely think I'd gotten enough already, considering the circumstances."

"I'm afraid he's right, Miss Richards. I'm sorry."

"I'm sorry, too." She looked up at him. "Just one more question and then I won't take up any more of your time." She smiled a little wanly. "Could Ben refuse to marry me?" she said, asking the question she hadn't dared to consider before now. She'd been so sure the will could be broken that she hadn't thought the question would be necessary.

"Refuse to marry you? I'm afraid I don't understand."

"The will says that I have six months to marry Ben or the ranch becomes completely his. But it says nothing about his having to marry me. I was wondering if he could stall for those six months and cheat me out of it altogether, even if I had made it clear that I was willing to marry him?"

Lyle Higgins looked down at the will, reading the clause in question and then reading it again.

"I'm afraid you're right, Miss Richards. Your grandfather's will doesn't specifically state that Mr. Oakes must marry you, but—" he glanced at it again "—it certainly implies it. I would say that your grandfather felt it unnecessary to bind his son by putting it in writing. He has merely assumed that his wishes would be carried out. That you would be allowed to choose." He looked at her closely. "Do you have reason to believe that Mr. Oakes won't honor his father's wishes?"

Stacey stood up, crushing out her cigarette as she did so. "I don't know," she said, picking up her copy of the will from the lawyer's desk. "I don't even know if I want to find out." She offered her hand. "Thank you for your time, Mr. Higgins," she said formally. "I appreciate your seeing me on such short notice. I'll be in touch if I decide to pursue the matter."

"I'm sorry that I couldn't be more encouraging, Miss Richards," he said as he ushered her to the door. "Please give André my best when you see him again."

"Yes, I'll do that." She smiled, but the smile faded as the door closed soundlessly behind her.

The long black limousine she'd hired was parked at the curb, waiting for her. The driver, John, moved hurriedly from his place behind the wheel at the sight of her and pulled open the rear passenger door. "Where to, Miss Richards?" he asked as she slid into the air-conditioned coolness of the back seat.

She considered the question as she rummaged almost frantically through her purse for her cigarette case, again without finding it. Where was the damn thing? Her fingers brushed a business card—Ben's. She turned it over slowly and read the address that he had scribbled on the back.

It was a North Dallas address in one of the new town house developments. He was here often enough, he'd said this morning when he gave it to her, to warrant having a permanent address. But she didn't want to go to Ben's town house. He might be there. And the less time she had to spend with him the better.

The plane ride this morning with just the two of them in the cockpit of the tiny Piper Cherokee had been bad enough. She should have known that Ben would pilot it himself and that there would be no third person to lessen the tension between them. It'd been just as uncomfortable as Stacey had feared it would be. Their conversation was abrupt and infrequent, focusing mainly on comments about the view. Ben didn't touch her except to hand her into and out of the plane, but Stacey could feel him watching her occasionally out of the corner of his eye. She'd refused to acknowledge even this brief contact and hunched her shoulders, turning to gaze out the side window as if transfixed by the flat landscape passing below them. But she could still feel his eyes touching her.

"Miss Richards?" the chauffeur asked again and Stacey looked up to find him watching her in the mirror.

She flushed, feeling as if she had been caught in some forbidden act. "Ah, have you got a cigarette?" she said. "I seem to have lost mine and I'm about to have a fit."

He extended a pack toward her, one long arm reaching over the back seat.

She pulled one from the offered pack. "Thank you." She lit it hurriedly and took a deep, calming drag. The strong tobacco burned as it went down but, magically, it seemed to steady her shaking fingers. *Great way to quit smoking*, she thought, *three cigarettes before lunch*.

"Decided where you'd like to go now, Miss Richards?" John asked then.

"Oh, yes. I'm sorry." Stacey fingered the card in her hand, rubbing her thumb across the embossed lettering on the front. She still didn't want to go to Ben's town house. "I want to go shopping," she decided suddenly. She'd mentioned that she wanted to do some shopping, hadn't she? Okay, she'd go shopping. "Let's try Neiman Marcus first," she said, stuffing Ben's business card back into her purse.

"Wait here, please," she instructed when the limo had pulled to a stop in front of the department store. "I'll meet you at this entrance in, oh, an hour and a half, two hours at the most," she said, sliding out of the car as John opened the door to assist her.

She walked quickly past the designer departments, headed determinedly toward sportswear. What was needed, she had already decided, were some casual clothes more appropriate to life on the ranch than the ones she'd brought with her. Quickly, she picked out three pairs of size eight Calvin Klein denim jeans, several Liz Claibourne and Gloria Vanderbilt tops in various styles and colors to go with both the jeans and the pants she'd brought with her, and an armload of cotton T-shirts in assorted colors.

Before she'd finished in the sportswear department she'd added three shorts-and-camisole-top playsuits, two bright cotton gauze sundresses by California designer Patti Cappalli and a big straw sun hat that she knew she'd never wear because she never wore hats. But she bought it, anyway.

Finished there, she headed toward the shoe department and bought six pairs of knee socks in bright solids, two pairs of canvas sneakers, white and navy, and two pairs of casual flat sandals by Beene Bag, both of which were absurdly expensive. "Done," she congratulated herself as she headed toward the exit.

But her eye was caught by an extravagant display in the lingerie department. She stopped short, causing at least two other shoppers to detour sharply to avoid careening into her. She had to spend at least one night, maybe two, alone with Ben in what she assumed was a small town house and all she had was that damned white silk gown and robe. Resolutely she searched out the most covered-up nightwear she could find.

Nothing the least suggestive about this, she thought with satisfaction as she paid for pale blue man-tailored pajamas and a full length navy blue robe of the finest wool. She politely declined the salesgirl's offer to have them monogrammed for her.

"Now where?" asked John as she deposited herself and her purchases in the back seat of the limo.

"Well, I need some boots," she said, still unwilling to chance running into Ben at the town house. If she stayed out long enough he was bound to be out by the time she got there. "What's the best Western-wear store in town these days?"

John considered a moment, looking at her in his rearview mirror, taking note of the expensive jewelry, the chic upswept hairdo, the large number of shopping bags with their exclusive Neiman Marcus label. "That would be The Wild Buffalo," he said. "Pretty steep, price-wise, though."

"But it's the best?"

"Yep."

"The Wild Buffalo it is, then," she said gaily, suddenly feeling as light-hearted as if she didn't have a care in the world beyond spending as much money as fast as humanly possible.

Thirty minutes later and several thousand dollars poorer, Stacey again tossed an armload of shopping bags into the back seat of the limo. She'd succumbed without a fight to the salesman's persuasion and purchased two pairs of boots, new riding gloves, a gray cowboy hat—cowboy hats being the one kind of hat she did wear—several pearl-snap Western-cut shirts and an extravagant and practically useless fur vest made of luxurious red fox with dozens of fox tails adorning the hem. She'd bought presents, too: a bronze paperweight in the shape of an oil derrick for André, engraved silver belt buckles, feathered hatbands and colorful Western bandanas to send to friends in Paris.

"Looks like more than boots," John commented with an indulgent grin.

Stacey nodded slowly and looked at the piles of packages heaped on the back seat and overflowing into the front with a rather dazed expression. She hardly remembered buying all that. She blinked as if waking up, suddenly realizing she'd been doing what she'd done those first years in Paris. Buying, always buying, as if trying to fill a void or solve her problems by throwing money around. The light-hearted feeling was gone in an instant, leaving her feeling drained and exhausted.

"Where to now?" asked John when her eyes met his in the rearview mirror.

"Home, I think, would be best," she said, giving him the address.

He helped her inside with her packages, thanked her for her generous tip and was gone. Stacey was left standing alone in the middle of Ben's cream-and-rust living room.

It was a nice room. The glass tables, high beamed ceiling and one wall of stereo and video equipment made it modern, and the pit sofa covered in rust-colored corduroy velvet, the brick fireplace, the plants and the paintings made it comfortable. But Stacey barely registered her surroundings.

She was aghast at the vast numbers of shopping bags and boxes spilling over the sofa cushions and onto the thick pile cream carpet. She'd spent literally thousands of dollars on things she had no earthly need for! What was happening to her, she asked herself. Where was all that self-control and cool common sense that André was always praising her for?

"A little shopping!" she said aloud, the sound of her own voice making her start nervously.

Almost guiltily she gathered up as many shopping bags as she could carry and hurried across the living room to an open doorway that looked as if it might lead to the bedrooms. She found herself in a short tiled hallway with three more doors opening off it. She peeked into the first room, catching a glimpse of thick sand-colored carpet.

"Ben?" she called softly, just to be sure. Getting no answer, she shouldered open the door and went in.

The room wasn't large but the sand-colored carpet was an extremely low pile, fine wool weave and covered the walls and the ceiling as well as the floor, giving the impression of an endless expanse of desert. Even the woodwork and the louvered doors of the closet all along one wall were painted the same color so that they blended in, defying the casual eye to guess at the real dimensions of the room.

There were only a few pieces of furniture and Stacey's gaze was drawn immediately to the king-size bed centered on the longest wall. It was covered with a heavy Indian blanket in jewel colors of turquoise, beige and coral. A huge hammered-brass Aztec sunburst hung on the wall above it in place of the more usual headboard. There were traditional Mexican leather-and-lattice tables on either side of the big bed. A rounded barrel chair of the same material sat in front of a parson's desk with burnished brass fittings.

She didn't need to see the slacks and shirt thrown carelessly across the foot of the bed or the size twelve-and-a-half cowboy boots on the floor beside it to tell her that this was Ben's bedroom. It was very much like him, she thought, extremely masculine, almost primitive, Western to the core. She backed hastily out of the room, as if Ben himself and not just his clothes were lying on the bed.

The next room she poked her nose into was a bathroom and the one after that another bedroom. A neutral room, neither overly masculine nor feminine, with a turquoise carpet and smooth cream walls. The tailored bedspread and drapes were made of matching fabric in a small geometric print in rust, cream and turquoise, as was the upholstered armchair in front of the window. Bleached wood bedside tables, a long, low dresser and an unusual wall mirror with a latticed frame made up the rest of the furnishings.

Stacey's suitcases sat unopened at the foot of the shiny brass bed. With a sigh of relief she kicked off her high-heeled pumps and dropped her packages on the floor. Then she hurried back into the living room for the rest of her purchases. She came to an abrupt halt just inside the doorway, her hand lifting automatically to stifle her gasp of surprise as Ben straightened and turned toward her, a piece of paper in his hand.

Stacey stood where she was, rooted to the spot, the fingers of one hand still touching her lips, her eyes wide. Never, she thought in that one shocked second, never had she seen such a beautiful man! He stood there on the cream carpet, his feet bare, like a statue cast in polished bronze, wearing only black swim trunks and a turquoise towel slung casually around his neck.

"I saw the limo pull up," he said, speaking first.

"Where were you?" was all she could manage. She felt like a gawky schoolgirl catching her first glimpse of a near-naked man. She hoped fervently that she wasn't blushing.

"Doing laps." He gestured over his shoulder toward the wall of windows behind him with their view of the swimming pool sparkling from across the width of the manicured lawn.

Stacey hadn't noticed the view when she came in and she barely glanced at it now. She was too busy watching the fascinating ripple of muscle under the thick pelt of chest hair as he gestured behind him. She remembered how it had curled around her fingers when she touched him and how it felt, rather coarse and crinkly, beneath her exploring hands. She yearned, with fierce intensity, to touch him again, and her eyes caressed the mat of black hair, following it to where it narrowed on his flat belly, curling around his exposed navel and then disappeared temptingly into the black swim trunks.

She saw the muscles of his stomach contract suddenly, tightening as if he'd abruptly sucked in his breath, and her eyes flew guiltily to his face, her own flaming hotly. She caught a brief look of fierce, unbridled desire in Ben's eyes before she tore her gaze away to focus blindly on the jumble of packages still on the sofa.

You came in here to get those, she told herself sternly. *So get them and get out. Get away. Quickly.*

She moved forward determinedly, her eyes fixed on the brightly colored packages, afraid if she looked up at Ben again, looked at that strong, gleaming body, into those fierce blue eyes, she would be lost forever. Carefully, she stepped around him and began picking up the rest of her packages.

He watched her walk around him, careful not to touch him in any way, and felt his guts twist. Was she that afraid of him? Or that disgusted by him? "Looks like you had a busy afternoon," he said, because he had to say something. His hand came into her field of vision, the receipt from The Wild Buffalo held out to her.

The feeling of guilt at her overindulgence came rushing back and, with it, irrational anger at Ben for making her feel that way. She welcomed both feelings gladly. They were better, far better, than the dangerous, delicious feelings that the sight of his lean, unclothed body had aroused in her.

"It's my money," she snapped, snatching the receipt from his fingers without looking up. "You had no right to pry!"

She felt his hand on her upper arm, detaining her when she would have turned away, back to the relative safety of the guestroom. "That was just a comment, honey," he said softly, reassuringly, as if she were a young animal that needed soothing. "Not a criticism. The receipt was lying on the floor and I picked it up. I'm sorry if you thought I was prying." His bare brown shoulders lifted in a shrug. "I was just curious, I guess, to see what kind of things you'd buy for yourself."

"They're not all for me," she said almost defensively, confused by this sudden change in mood that she sensed in him.

"No," he agreed absently, wondering at her defensive tone, and then, "Let's call a truce, shall we, Stacey? At least for tonight."

"A truce?" she echoed hesitantly.

"All this fencing and feinting around each other." He paused and ran a hand through his damp, curling hair. "I'll make reservations somewhere for dinner. We'll eat out, in public, like two old friends. We'll forget about the other night, the ranch, Henry's damn will. We'll talk instead of jumping down each other's throat." He looked down at her and smiled hopefully. "How does that sound to you? Truce?"

"That sounds fine," she agreed slowly, except that, strangely enough, she didn't want to be his friend, not anymore. Not when her pulses were racing madly out of control at just the sight of him. She couldn't forget the other night, even if he could. But he was right. They had to talk. Really talk. "Truce," she said.

"Good." He dropped her arm then, already heading for the telephone. "You can have the bathroom first," he said as he dialed. "I'll give you an hour's head start."

10

THE RESTAURANT he took her to was an elegant private club housed in what had once been someone's home—if something so huge could be called a home—in the exclusive Turtle Creek area of Dallas. It was the area where the city's very oldest money still lived.

The Cipango Club, Ben told her as they turned into the curved, porticoed driveway, had at one time been an exclusive and illicit gambling establishment with bootleg liquor and rooms available upstairs. It was also said that during the same time a gentleman never brought his own wife to dine and play at the club except on New Year's Eve. Or so the legend went. Whether it was true was anybody's guess.

In any case, it was an entirely respectable club now, and wives were allowed anytime, he smilingly informed her.

Happily, the club had managed to retain a great deal of the glamour and ambience of that earlier, more reckless era. A pretty receptionist in a long evening dress sat at a desk just inside the door to check memberships and reservations. She didn't even glance at her book when Ben stopped at her desk. "Good evening, Mr. Oakes," she said, her smile warmer than was strictly necessary. "Would you like to be seated in the dining room immediately, or would you prefer to go into the bar first?"

"The dining room, please, Cassie," he said, and she smiled again, extending her arm gracefully to motion them into the main lobby and from there into the dining room.

The appointments were quietly lush and faintly art deco with a fireplace and a cushioned sofa and armchairs in the mirrored lobby and extravagant arrangements of fresh flowers throughout. As they stepped up into the main lobby Stacey caught sight of their reflection in the mirrored walls. For just a brief instant, she thought she was looking at another couple.

What a stunning pair, she thought in that moment before she realized that the blue eyes looking back at her were her own. *Well, we do make a stunning couple,* she insisted to herself. Her own image was slender and pale in a black silk sheath of a dress that left her shoulders and arms totally bare. Her skin seemed to have the sheen of a pearl, gleaming in the low lights that reflected off the mirrors and sparkled on the diamond-studded hoops in her ears.

Ben, so tall and dark beside her, stood head and shoulders over her own not insignificant height even in her highest black heels. He looked magnificent in a pale gray, summer-weight suit and immaculate gray cowboy boots. His crisp white shirt only served to emphasize the swarthiness of his skin and the midnight black of his hair where it just touched the collar in back. His tie was silk, an elegant gray-and-scarlet stripe. He looked totally correct and appropriate for the occasion, but it seemed to Stacey as if his rampant masculinity was only intensified by the sophisticated clothes he wore and the refined atmosphere in which he found himself. It was a masculinity that served to enhance and emphasize her own femininity.

Never, she thought, had she looked so fragile and so female as she did now, standing next to Ben while he exchanged pleasantries with the tuxedoed maître d'.

"Stacey?" Ben said softly. His hand at the small of her back urged her forward, and she came out of her daze to follow the maître d' to their table.

After they ordered drinks from a waiter who identified himself as Mark, they sat silently.

Stacey gazed around her, wondering what to say. Talk, he'd said. Like old friends, he'd said. Well, what did old friends talk about? Old times? Common interests? No, old times for them were a touchy subject, and as for common interests, well, what did they have in common except the ranch and Henry? She stole a look at him through her lowered lashes. The ranch and Henry she amended, and that hot, almost painfully sweet feeling that flamed so easily, too easily, between them.

"This is a lovely place," she said finally. "So elegant. I didn't expect—"

"You didn't expect it in a hick place like Texas?" he interrupted, "or you didn't expect a hick like me to know about it?"

Her eyes flew up to his, genuinely contrite. "Oh, no, that's not what I meant at all!" she began, but he was smiling at her, a teasing glint in his blue eyes. "All right, yes," she said, smiling back at him. "That's what I meant. But I take it back. Texas isn't a hick place, or at least Dallas isn't and—" her lashes fluttered down and then up again "—neither are you," she said softly.

"Well, thank you for that," he said lightly, but the look in his eyes was anything but light. Their eyes held for a heartbeat or two, each seeking something from the other, asking questions that as yet had no answers.

"May I offer the lady a rose?" asked another waiter at Ben's elbow.

Ben nodded his assent, his eyes never leaving Stacey's, and for a confused moment she thought his nod was meant to agree with whatever she'd just silently asked him. She felt herself begin to color delicately and then the waiter came between them, presenting her with a single, perfect red rose theatrically offered on a small satin pillow. She reached for it, breaking eye contact with Ben, and brought it to her nose, inhaling the sweet, heady fragrance.

"For the rose," the waiter said, setting a crystal bud vase on the table and then Mark appeared at her other side with her aperitif, offering the menus and his own recommendations for their meal.

Ben turned to the waiter, after asking Stacey's preferences, and ordered for both of them. The wine steward appeared as Mark retreated and another few minutes were spent in earnest discussion over the wine list.

"Does that meet with your approval?" Ben asked as he handed the leather-covered wine list back to the sommelier.

"Yes, that's fine," Stacey said, though she had no idea what he had ordered.

"Good." He leaned forward, both elbows on the table, one big hand idly twisting his bourbon glass on the snowy cloth. "Tell me about your life in Paris," he said conversationally. He'd wanted to know for a long, long time.

"There's nothing much to tell. I work." Stacey shrugged delicately. "I live."

"There's eleven years' worth," Ben said.

She laughed softly, though there was nothing funny in what he had said. "Yes," she said and began to tell him about boarding school and business school. She described her apartment and her job, telling him how much she enjoyed working for André's oil company and about their trips to Saudi Arabia and, laughingly, about the sheik who'd once tried to purchase her favors. Consciously or unconsciously she painted a rosy picture, leaving out the loneliness and the homesickness and the years of hurt.

"Your turn," she said when she'd run out of things she could, or would, tell him.

He answered her queries about his life in the same way, telling her about the improvements he had brought to the ranch; about his race horses and the Santa Gertrudis cattle he was breeding; about the small, experimental herd of buffalo being raised, he hoped, for market. He talked about the modern windmills she'd seen on her drive to the main house, about the "helicopter herding" and Pete's disgust with it, and about the land he'd loaned to some Texas Tech college students who were convinced that a common desert weed was the answer to the nation's alternative energy problems.

"Who knows?" he laughed. "Maybe they're right. And if they are I want to be one of the first to know about it."

"I'm sure you will be," Stacey agreed.

They kept up their informative, if light-hearted, conversation all through the escargot appetizers and the tossed salad with its delicious blue cheese dressing. They paused for a few minutes for the small ritual of the wine tasting and then laughed together like children at the obvious disapproval of the sommelier over Ben's choice; a compromise rosé to compliment both Ben's Steak Diane and Stacey's sauteed red snapper in lemon sauce.

Neither of them mentioned Henry or the will or what they were going to do about it. She didn't mention any men, except quite casually in passing, though there'd been two who'd been important to her at different times in her life. He didn't mention women, either, though she knew that in eleven years there must have been two or three. She studied him appreciatively, toying with her wineglass as she listened to him expound authoritatively on the subject of oil and energy. Probably, she thought, suppressing a stab of jealousy, the women in his life numbered more like five or six. If not more.

The meal was over more quickly than she could believe and they sat there with their coffee, watching silently as their waiter made a small, pleasant production of warming their brandy in the big crystal snifters. He set them on the table with a flourish and then offered Ben a cigar to properly cap the meal.

"Do you mind?" Ben asked Stacey, his hand poised over the open humidor.

"Nasty habit," she teased, smiling her assent, and he grinned at her.

"Smoke if you want to," he said magnanimously.

"Gee, thanks," Stacey drawled, letting him know with her eyes and her tone of voice that she hadn't forgotten his reaction the last time she'd smoked in his presence, and that she was amused by his condescending offer to let her do so now. "But I've either lost or misplaced my cigarette case and I had a couple of American cigarettes already today. They tasted rather awful." She shrugged expressively. "I can forgo it."

"If you'll excuse me," interrupted the waiter, "we carry Gauloises cigarettes."

"Really? That would be lovely," she said, and Mark hurried off to get them for her.

"He knew you were French," Ben said, eyeing her speculatively over the snifter of brandy. Smoke from the cigar held in the same hand drifted between them.

"But I'm not French. I'm a Texan," she objected.

"You look French. Especially when you give that little shrug. No American woman—no. No Texas woman," he amended, "moves quite that way. I don't mean it as a criticism. I like it," he said when she looked about to speak, belatedly realizing he did like it—very much. "It makes you different." His voice dropped intimately. "Mysterious."

He looked away from her as the waiter appeared at his elbow. "Thank you, Mark," he said, taking the pack of cigarettes. "I'll take care of it." He placed a cigarette between his lips, lighting it with the burning end of his cigar. He took it from his mouth with two fingers, turning his wrist, and held it against her closed lips.

"Take it," he ordered softly and it was as if he had said *Kiss me* instead.

Stacey took it between her lips and inhaled, feeling as if she could taste his mouth on the burning cigarette, knowing it was impossible. Her hand came up to take it from his fingers. "Thank you," she murmured shakily. She glanced down nervously at the pack of Gauloises lying on the table, at the black matchbook with the gold lettering, the coffee cups and brandy snifters and Ben's hands, brown and strong against the white tablecloth and the even whiter cuffs of his shirt. He held the cigar lightly between his first two fingers in the American way.

"Ben," she said, "we have to talk." It couldn't be put off any longer, could it? They *had* to talk. She had to tell him what the lawyer had said about breaking the will. And she had to tell him what she was going to do now.

He made a dismissive little movement with the hand holding the cigar. "We are talking."

"Ben, please don't make this any more difficult than it has to be." She glanced up at him quickly and then down again just as quickly, unable t read his eyes. "I saw a lawyer today," she began, hesitant but determined, "and he said that I . . . that you . . ." She floundered.

"He said that there was no way out, didn't he?" Ben said in a low voice. "For either of us." His voice was hard, grating against her ears, and her eyes flew to his face.

He didn't really want to marry her, she realized, despite what he'd said the other night. He didn't want to be forced into it any more than she did. He was trapped, too, by Henry's will. Trapped by the love he'd felt for his adoptive father and his adopted home.

"So you see why we have to talk?" she whispered.

"Yes," he agreed, dreading it, "but later. Not now. We have a truce for tonight, remember?" He laid his cigar in an ashtray. "No discussion of Henry and his damned will allowed." He stood up and held out his hand. "Dance with me," he ordered and then added when she hesitated, "Please?"

Silently, unable to resist him, not even wanting to resist him, Stacey crushed out her cigarette and put her hand in his, allowing him to draw her with him onto the dance floor. She tried to hold herself stiffly at first, keeping a sane few inches between them. Ben seemed to acquiesce, clasping his big hands loosely at the small of her back, but she soon realized that his casual hold on her was just as intimate, if not more so, than if he'd held her tightly to him. She could feel his eyes on her face, touching her bare neck and shoulders and the deep, shadowy cleft between her breasts.

Her own hands rested rather uneasily on his chest and she kept her eyes fixed determinedly on his striped tie and his snowy white shirtfront, refusing to look up. The shirt was so fine that, this close, she could see the faint shadow of the dark chest hair under it and feel the heat of his skin beneath her fingers. *Trust Ben*, she thought, with a faint, secret smile, *not to be wearing something so mundane as an undershirt.*

"Let me in on the joke?" he whispered, wondering what had caused that small, catlike smile to curve her lips.

She could feel his warm, brandy-scented breath stir the fine, wispy hairs at her temple. "You're not wearing an undershirt," she said without thinking about it first. If she had she might have realized how aware of him it revealed her to be.

He grinned. Somehow, without looking up into his face, she knew that. "Neither are you," he teased, and she felt his eyes run over her again, touching her face and hair and her smooth bare shoulders.

Her hand went to her neck as if to cover the bruise there, though it was now so faint that a dab of concealing cream had hidden it completely. He didn't seem to notice her instinctive, protective reaction to his wandering gaze.

"In fact," he continued, "you don't look as if you're wearing much of anything. Not that I'm complaining." His arms loosened a fraction and his eyes ran the length of her slender figure. He sighed theatrically. "The men of the world owe a great debt of gratitude to French designers," he said and then, as if it had just occurred to him. "That is French, isn't it?"

"Yes," she nodded, wondering vaguely where all this was leading to. "St. Laurent."

"Uh-huh. Thought so," he said, and she finally looked up at him through her lashes and was startled by the look in his eyes. They were hot—burning hot—and hungry, completely at odds with the light, almost playful, conversation they were having.

"Dance," he said softly and she realized she'd stopped moving to stare up at him, her own eyes mirroring, had she but known it, the expression burning in his. "Stop looking at me like that and dance," he whispered, his voice ragged. His words were no longer playful.

Her eyes fell swiftly, protectively, afraid of what she might have revealed to him in that brief glance. His arms tightened around her, pulling her close. She didn't resist.

Yes, she thought, turning her face into his shoulder, hiding from him and from herself. Yes, it was better this way, dancing sightless and silently. She couldn't give herself away if he couldn't see her face, she thought, if he couldn't see the unwilling, unwanted love burning in her eyes. *Oh, Ben,* she almost cried aloud, *I don't want to love you. I don't!*

"I've tried to fight it," he whispered raggedly against her ear.

For a crazy moment she thought she'd spoken aloud and that he was answering her. But, no, it wasn't love he had to fight.

"I thought I could control it," he continued, his voice low and harsh, "but I can't, I never could! I just look at you . . . see you standing there so cool and remote and so incredibly beautiful and I want you again. More than I've ever wanted anything." His hands shifted, cupping her shoulders to hold her a little away from him so that he could look down into her face. His own was harsh and tortured as she stared up at him. "Do you realize what it's cost me to admit that? Can you imagine what it does to my self-respect to know I can't keep my hands off you?" His fingers dug into her shoulders almost painfully.

She shook her head in denial, hardly aware that she did so. No, it wasn't love he fought, it was lust. He wanted her and he hated himself for wanting her.

"And then the other night, when we made love, it was so incredibly good. So..." He shook his head as if to clear it and his hands slid slowly down her arms to clasp her fingers in his, crushing them in his anguished grasp. "It only made me want you more," he said. "Now that I know how you are, how you look...." One hand came up to touch her face and his eyes held hers for what seemed like endless seconds, searching. "How you respond when you're naked in my arms."

Stacey caught her breath at that, gasping audibly for air, her eyes wide with unwilling arousal. As much as he might despise himself for wanting her, she despised herself even more for responding so hungrily to the heat in his eyes. A heat she knew, because he'd just told her, that was backed by nothing but lust. And yet, even knowing that, her single most driving impulse at the moment was to turn her lips into the hand touching her cheek and tickle his palm with her tongue. Fighting him, fighting herself, she turned her face away.

His hand dropped and she heard a sound from him like a ragged sigh, but she wasn't sure. "Let's get out of here," he said, his voice low and fierce, "before I make an even bigger fool of myself than I already have." Placing his hand at the small of her back, he steered her to their table.

So, wanting her made him a fool, did it? Then what, she wondered, did loving him make her?

"Will there be anything else, Mr. Oakes?" asked Mark, the perfect waiter, appearing at the table as if by magic.

"Just the check," Ben said shortly.

As he signed it, adding a generous tip, Stacey shakily gathered up her tiny satin evening bag, stuffing the cigarettes into it, and turned toward the lobby, leaving Ben to follow behind her. If she could have left without making a scene, called a cab or walked back to the town house, she would have. But the pretty receptionist was watching her, rather enviously she realized, and Ben was just behind her. She pushed open the outer door, needing to keep as much space between them as possible, needing to keep away from the heat of his big body—and keep him from feeling the heat in her own.

"Miss . . . ma'am," she heard the waiter's voice behind her. "Your rose."

She turned and reached for the flower automatically, a stiff smile of thanks curving her lips and then nodded another thank-you as the valet held open the car door for her. She didn't say a word on the short drive back to the town house and neither did Ben. She sat stiffly, clutching the rose tightly in one hand as if it were a lifeline. She wanted a cigarette, but she was trembling so badly that she was afraid she wouldn't be able to light it.

It's okay, she told herself, *you'll be there soon and you can lock yourself in the bedroom and smoke the whole damned pack.*

"Stacey? We're here."

She heard Ben's voice as if from a long way away, and like an automaton, she reached for the door handle and pushed it open. Ben came swiftly around the car and she felt his hand on her elbow, guiding her up the walkway and onto the well-lit porch of the town house. She heard the click of his key in the lock, then the door was open, the soft diffused track lights were snapped on, her purse was taken from her. She knew she was behaving strangely, like a sleepwalker, but she couldn't seem to help it. Only by blocking out all emotion, all aware- ness, could she keep from throwing herself into Ben's arms and begging him to take what was already his, what had always been his.

"Let go," she heard him say.

She looked down as both his hands covered one of hers. She still clutched the rose and it was that that Ben wanted her to release. She opened her fingers, letting him take it from her. She'd been clutching it so tightly that a lone thorn had imbedded itself in the soft pad of flesh at the base of her thumb.

She blinked like someone waking from a dream as Ben raised her wounded hand to his mouth and pulled out the tiny thorn with his teeth. "They're supposed to be thornless hybrids," he said. The words were light, but the tone wasn't. "I'll have to speak to Mark." Then, having disposed of the thorn, he gently kissed the spot where it had been.

His lips were warm against her palm for several sec- onds and she could feel the firm, hard line of his jaw un- der her passive fingers. "Don't," she said then, trying to pull her hand away.

Ben held on to it for a brief second longer, filled with indecision, and then he dropped it and turned abruptly away from her. "I'm going to have a brandy," he said, his voice weary. He opened a bar that was cleverly con- cealed in the wall of electronic equipment. "How about you?" He half turned, the brandy decanter in his hand.

"No, I'm going to bed," she said hesitantly. "I—"

"You were right, Stacey," he interrupted, loath to let her go just yet. "We need to talk."

"Yes," she sighed wearily. They did need to talk. They couldn't go on like this, constantly sparring with each other, advancing and retreating. Although what good talking would do them, she didn't know.

She went to sit in the farthest corner of the pit sofa, kicked off her high-heeled shoes and curled her legs up under her protectively, her hands clasped over her bent knees. She didn't reach for the drink that Ben held out to her, but made a little motion with her head, indicating to him that he should set it down on the glass coffee table.

She was scared to touch him, she admitted to herself, even so casually and impersonally. Scared that she wouldn't be able to talk, not reasonably, if she touched him.

He took a large swallow of his drink and set it down on the table next to hers. Then he stripped off his suit coat, tossing it carelessly over an arm of the sofa and one big hand came up, tugging loose his tie and unbuttoning the top two buttons of his shirt as he sank onto the sofa near her.

"So?" he said, reaching for his glass again with one hand, handing hers across to her with the other. She took it carefully, avoiding contact with his fingers. "You saw your lawyer today," he stated. "Now what happens?"

She took a sip of her drink, buying time. "I don't know." And it was true, she didn't. She'd been so sure before she'd seen the lawyer, positive that Henry's will could be easily broken. And now, finding out that it was probably going to take an unsavory court battle, she was uncertain and afraid. "I just don't know."

Ben sighed, leaning his head back against the sofa cushions, eyes closed. He was so damned tired. Of everything; the ranch, Henry's will, fighting himself, fighting her, wanting and not having. "Well, what advice did your lawyer give you?" He opened his eyes and looked at her.

She looked into her glass. "You know what he said. The same thing you did. That it would take a court case. And that no Texas jury could be counted on to see my side of it, not unless I . . ." She shrugged and then stilled the movement guiltily, remembering how he said it made her look—different and mysterious and foreign. "I'm not Texan enough anymore, I guess," she said, unwilling to tell him all the unpleasant details of what the lawyer had said.

"Not unless what?" he prompted.

She shrugged again, staring down into her brandy glass as if it held all the secrets of the universe.

"Come on, Stacey, you might as well tell me and get it over with."

She took a deep sip of her drink and then brought it to her lap, cradling it between her palms. "He said that I'd either have to prove that we were really related by blood or—"

"Which we're not."

"—or, I'd have to convince the jury that I've always thought of you as my real uncle and that I . . . that I'd feel incestuous at any thought of an . . . intimate relationship with you."

"And do you?"

She took another sip of her drink. "No," she admitted softly.

Ben let out a breath he didn't know he'd been holding. "So where does that leave us?"

"I don't know." She hesitated, waiting for him to say something.

He just continued looking at her, waiting for her to go on.

"I guess it means we end up in court," she said slowly, feeling compelled to answer him. "Where all I have to do is convince a jury that I've always believed Henry was your real father."

"Henry *was* my real father," Ben said forcefully. "He just wasn't my biological father. Some no-account rodeo cowboy was my real father."

"How do you know that?"

His hesitation was so brief as to be nonexistent. Telling her would be breaking a confidence that even Henry hadn't been a party to but she had to know. He wanted her to know. "I know because Marta told me," he said. "And Marta would know because she's my mother."

Stacey's eyes widened. "Marta's your mother?" she whispered. "*Our* Marta?"

"Yes, our Marta."

"But how? Why? I don't understand."

"What's to understand? She was sixteen and pregnant by a cowboy who told her he loved her, then took off as soon as he found out there was going to be a baby. Abortion was out because of her religion and—"

Stacey gasped. "Not abortion," she protested, aghast at the thought of there never being a Ben.

"No," he agreed, "not abortion. Adoption. Of a sort," he added wearily.

"Of a sort?" Stacey prompted when he didn't immediately continue.

"Her older sister, Elena, was married to an Anglo rancher in New Mexico," he said quietly, staring into his glass. "Six years married, but there weren't any children, and Elena was desperate for a child." He swirled the liquid in his glass, watching it as if the sight fascinated him. "It seemed like the ideal solution at the time," he said, repeating what Marta had told him all those years ago. "One that was supposed to solve everybody's problem. My mother wouldn't be forced to give up her child to strangers, I'd never have to know I was illegitimate, and Elena would save her marriage. But it didn't work out that way." He lifted the glass to his lips and took a deep swallow, relishing the burning as it went down. "My *father*—" his lip curled at the word "—couldn't reconcile himself to the fact that someone else's bastard was the only son he was ever going to have, but he couldn't quite bring bring himself to refute me, either."

"Oh, Ben." Compassion gripped her heart and stung her eyes at the thought of all the pain his few words encompassed. For him. For Marta. For Elena. And even for Elena's husband. "Ben." Her hand came up to touch his face. "I'm so sorry. It must have been awful for you."

He shrugged away from her touch, uncomfortable with her pity. He didn't want pity from Stacey. He never had. "It wasn't fun," he admitted. "But it was over a long time ago."

"I'm still sorry," she said.

"Yeah, well..." He upended his drink, draining it, then reached out and set it on the glass-topped coffee table. "So where do we go from here, Stacey?"

He knew as well as she did that she wouldn't be taking it to court now. Marta was the only mother she'd ever known. The woman who'd bandaged her scraped knees and seen that she'd done her homework and explained the mysteries of her changing body. She'd never do anything to hurt Marta.

And having it known that she'd borne a child out of wedlock would hurt her deeply because, though an illegitimate baby might not be a big thing to most people these days, it would be to Marta, who still went to Mass twice a week.

Marta had made her decision years ago, Stacey thought. She'd given up her baby to be raised by another woman, she'd left her home to avoid bringing shame on her family, she'd denied herself the pleasure and pride of declaring Ben her son to all the world, even when that world would no longer condemn her. On top of all that, she'd lived with all the guilt and doubts and pain her decisions had certainly brought her. For Stacey to challenge it now, to bring it out in the open for everyone to comment over, would be the worst sort of betrayal.

So, no matter how much she wanted the ranch, no matter how desperately she craved to own a part of her childhood home, she couldn't go after it at Marta's expense. Which meant, unless Ben was willing to just give it to her with no strings attached, she'd have to walk away from it. Again.

"Stacey?"

"I guess—" her voice trembled "—I guess it's up to you," she said. She twisted the brandy glass in her hand, swirling the amber liquid against the sides of the snifter as he'd done just a moment ago.

"The decision is yours," he said firmly. He wasn't going to force her into anything. Not again. Not ever again.

"I can't," she said, realizing it was true. She couldn't make the decision. It was asking too much of her. She wanted him to make the decision for both of them. She wanted him to take the responsibility out of her hands. She wanted, she realized, for him to say that he loved her. Needed her. Wanted to marry her.

But she knew he wasn't going to.

"The decision is yours," he repeated. "Henry wanted it that way."

Stacey nodded, her eyes closed. *Yes, Henry,* she thought. But what, really, had Henry wanted? Had he intended that she should say yes to Ben? Or had he wanted her to say no?

"Stacey?" He extended a tentative hand toward her.

She shot up suddenly, slamming her glass down on the tabletop. "Don't push me, Ben," she said, half pleading, half commanding. "I don't know. I just don't know!"

"Are you going to drag this out for the whole six months, then?"

"No! I couldn't stand that!"

"Then make a decision!" He reached for her hand again, pulling her back down on the sofa. "What do you want, Stacey?"

You, she wanted to say, as the touch of his hand ignited her, *just you.* She should have pulled away then but she didn't. Couldn't.

"The ranch?" he persisted relentlessly. "Or Paris?"

Were those her only choices? The ranch or Paris and nothing in between?

"I . . ." She hesitated uncertainly. Her whole future depended on her next words. Could she tell him what she wanted? Could she bare her pride that far and trust that he wouldn't trample on it? "I want the ranch," she said. Her voice was low, a mere thread of sound, but surprisingly firm.

"Even if I go with it? And I *do* go with it, Stacey, make no mistake about that," he said, wanting her to say that what she really wanted was him and to hell with the ranch. "Is that what you want?"

"I want the ranch," she said again, too full of pride and left-over hurt feelings to admit the real truth.

"All right." He yanked her into his arms. "All right, Stacey, let's see what we have to look forward to for the rest of our lives."

She went into his arms without a struggle, without a whimper of protest and lifted her open mouth to his descending one. *So what if it's only lust on his part*, she asked herself as their mouths fused and their tongues engaged in a passionate ballet, she had love enough for two. Plenty of marriages, good solid marriages, had been founded on far less. She could teach him to love her. He wanted her desperately, she could tell. Surely it was only a tiny step from that wanting to love. She *could* make him love her.

She felt his hand in her hair, loosening the pins so that it fell in heavy waves to her shoulders. His lips left off their exploration of her eager mouth to press moist, hungry kisses along her cheeks and jaw to her ear.

"I love to take your hair down," he whispered raggedly. "It's like messing up a prim little lady and turning her into a tigress." His tongue circled her ear and she quivered, her nails pressing into his shoulder. He thrilled to that small sign of her desire. "Or a wildcat," he said then. "My wildcat."

He pulled back a little to look into her face. Her hair was spread in wild disarray over his arm and shoulder, her eyes were smoldering, half closed with passion, her lips were red and slightly parted. He ran the tip of one finger slowly from her nose, down across her parted lips, to her chin and along the long slender line of her throat and chest to close possessively over one full breast. "Are you my wildcat, Stacey?" he asked huskily, his eyes roving over the seductive splendor of her flushed face.

"Yes." The word was almost inaudible. Her hand came up, pressing his to the warm, wanting curve of her breast. "Yes, Ben, I—" But she got no further.

She heard him take a deep, ragged breath, felt his fingers curve around her breast, kneading, and then somehow, in one smooth motion he managed to turn her pliant body so that she lay on the sofa. His long, hard length pressed her into the cushions. She welcomed his weight holding her down, welcomed his tongue as it once again sought entrance to the sweet, moist recesses of her mouth, welcomed the feel of his big, warm hand as he nudged aside the top of her dress to caress the swollen breast beneath.

"At least I can make you want me," he said into the warmth of her skin.

Stacey arched her body and her arms cradled him close, urging his moist, eager mouth to her breast. She wanted to tell him, over and over, that he didn't *make* her want him because she couldn't help wanting him. Just as she couldn't help loving him. But something held her back. Pride, stubbornness, the need to hear him say it first, to commit himself before she did.... Something.

"Stacey," he moaned. "Stacey, honey, I want you." His voice was muffled against her throat. His movements against her were almost frantic, his hands avid and greedy. "Say you want me, too, Stacey." He pressed his hips against her, letting her feel his raging desire and need. "Say it."

But she couldn't.

It would be the same as the last time, she thought. They'd make love frantically, like passionate, starving animals and then, afterward, when there should be closeness and sharing and whispered endearments, there'd be... She didn't know what there would be.

Nothing, probably. Shame. Uneasiness. Anger. Wary distrust. She couldn't take that again. Not ever again. Not from Ben.

Her body went lax beneath his. "Let me up." She pushed his chest when he didn't immediately release her. "Ben, let me up."

He stilled, his body tensing, his arms hard around her, unable to believe what he'd heard. He raised his head slightly. "Stacey?"

"Let me up," she repeated. "Please."

Her eyes were closed. Her body passive beneath his except for the slender hands pressing against his chest. *Like yesterday.* He'd gone after her like an animal again, he thought, disgusted with himself. He'd mauled her. Manhandled her. Hurt her. She must think he was some kind of crazed beast. He pushed himself up and off her, filled with self-loathing. "I'm sorry, Stacey."

She sat up slowly, pulling her dress up over her breasts. "Don't be," she said, her head down. "You can't help how you feel any more than I can."

"Stacey," he said, anguished. "I—"

"Please, don't apologize." She had to get away from him now, before she gave in again, before she threw herself into his arms and begged him to finish what they'd started. She stood. "If you'll excuse me," she said with admirable calm, for which she was ever after proud of herself. "It's been a long day and I'd like to go to bed." Her eyes met his briefly. "Alone."

He stepped back and let her pass him. There was nothing else to say. Nothing else to do.

She left the room with her head held high, picking up her purse and the now-wilting rose as she went. She managed to keep up her calm facade until the bedroom door closed quietly behind her. Then she turned the lock, dropping her shoes and purse and the faded flower on the carpet. Her whole body slumped and shrank inward as if she'd been hit in the stomach. Her arms came up to hug her upper body protectively.

This is what it would be like if I stayed, she thought. She was a fool to think she could make him love her. A fool! Oh, it might work for a while. He would probably be faithful as long as he still hungered for her body. But inevitably, there would come a day when someone else— someone like Linda Montoya, perhaps—would come along and he'd fall in love.

And when that happened she would surely die.

So she couldn't stay. No matter how much she wanted to, she just couldn't. The ranch didn't matter now, if it ever really had. All that mattered was Ben. She loved him too much to marry him and then have to watch him drift away from her. And he would. Eventually. She was sure of it.

If he loved her just a little she might have stood a chance of keeping him. But he didn't love her. He only wanted her, and that wasn't good enough.

She bent over and picked up her evening bag, finding and lighting a cigarette, and sat down on the edge of the brass bed, waiting for the soothing rush of smoke to work its magic and stop the shaking of her fingers enough so that she could use the telephone.

"André," she said calmly when she had made the connection. There was no trace of tears in her voice. "There's been a change of plans here and I'm returning to Paris after all. Do you think there's a chance I could have my old job back?"

ALONE IN THE LIVING ROOM Ben sat in the dark, drinking himself into insensibility in an effort to drown out the pain of losing her all over again. He'd thought it had hurt the first time, when he'd been little more than a boy in a man's body. But he'd been wrong. The second time around was far worse. Because now he knew just exactly what he was losing.

11

ANDRE WAS OVERJOYED to be getting back his beautiful and efficient assistant. Stacey had known he would be. He hadn't had time, in the few days she'd been gone, to even begin looking for someone to replace her.

"Not that it would be possible, *chérie*," he said gallantly, "because you are irreplaceable. But I am puzzled. You were so adamant about staying on your ranch. I despaired of ever seeing you again."

"I just changed my mind, André," she answered him. "Texas and the ranch just aren't my cup of tea anymore. And I missed Paris—and you too, of course—terribly."

That, in essence, was what she planned to tell Ben the next morning when she finally emerged from her bedroom with her suitcases already packed and a taxi summoned by phone.

He was standing in front of the stove with his back to her, his calves and feet bare beneath the hem of a white terry robe. His hair was damp, as if he'd just showered. There was a glass of tomato juice on the counter beside him and the smell of coffee permeated the air like strong perfume. He'd apparently weathered the night with no ill effects—unlike her. Stacey took a deep breath, fixed a cool smile on her face and walked into the room.

"Would you like some eggs?" he asked without turning around.

"Just coffee, thanks," she said, trying to sound breezily insouciant as she reached for the glass coffeepot on the counter. "I haven't got time for anything else."

"Haven't got time?" He turned around to look at her, a spatula in one hand, a pan of scrambled eggs in the other. His bare chest peeked out from between the loosely crossed lapels on his robe. His jaw was unshaven. His bloodshot eyes narrowed as he took in her polished appearance. "Are you going someplace?"

She busied herself with pouring out a cup of coffee. "Home," she said, as if it were the most natural thing in the world to say.

Ben put the spatula in the frying pan and set them both on the counter with no thought for the tiled surface. "Home? To the ranch?" he asked.

"Home." Her eyes flickered to his for a brief instant and then went back to the sugar she was stirring into her coffee. "To Paris."

Something twisted in his gut. "Paris?"

"Yes." She lifted the cup to her lips and took a quick sip. She'd put too much sugar in it. "I've decided that I just couldn't stand to live on the ranch," she said coolly, so intent on her hiding her true emotions that she couldn't see his for what they were. "You helped me make up my mind actually. Dinner last night and...everything. That lovely little club reminded me of just what I'd be giving up. And for what?" She shrugged and took another sip of the too sweet coffee. "A piece of dry desert land and half a herd of dirty cattle?" She shook her head as if at her own brief folly. "I decided it just wasn't worth it," she lied. "I mean really, Ben, can you honestly see me living at Iron Oakes, in that old-fashioned barn of a house, with Uncle Pete and all those hick hands?" She could see the anger building in his eyes, the anger and something else, but she refused to be deterred. "Married to *you*? Way out in the boonies with so few of the luxuries of life and no culture to speak of, after the way I've lived?"

She shrugged again deliberately, dismissively, subtly drawing his attention to the beautifully cut raw silk slacks, the soft silk blouse and the high-heeled snake-skin shoes, all in the same shade of deep forest green. A gold buckled snakeskin belt encircled her slim waist, gold hoops were in her ears and two fine gold chains, one with a diamond studded nugget, adorned her white throat. Her hair was swept up into a sleek coil, not a strand out of place, and she wore her new fox fur vest over all.

Its luxurious reddish color, the profusion of dangling tails at the hem, the basic impracticality of it made her look, she knew, sophisticated, spoiled and frivolous. Very much, in fact, as if she'd never in her entire life been near, or wanted to be near, anything so mundane as a cattle ranch.

No, he thought, *I really can't see Stacey on the ranch. Not this Stacey.*

"I'd get restless for the bright lights, the art galleries, the fabulous shopping . . ." She shrugged again and tried a careless little laugh, managing it quite well, she thought, despite the fact that it sounded a bit shrill. "Do you know, I haven't even had a decent croissant since I left home?"

She paused as if waiting for an answer, but he just stood there, staring at her with that bland, blank look on his face. As if, she thought, he was waiting for her to fin-ish saying whatever it was she felt she had to say so he could go back to his breakfast.

"And besides, there's André," she said, pride alone driving her now. Her words were intended to show him that what had happened between them meant as little to her as it obviously had to him. "Uncle Pete was right, you know. About what he said in the den that day. I do have a man in Paris, a lover. I thought I could leave him but—" again that maddening little shrug that made him want to strangle her "—I find that I can't."

He could feel the veins throbbing in his temples, pounding out the measured beat of his blood as if it were flowing out of him. He could feel his heart begin to crack. But he pressed his lips together and said nothing. Because, he thought, if he said anything at all he'd end up begging her to stay. And he wasn't quite reduced to that. Yet.

Stacey's fingers curled around the coffee cup in her hand, waiting. Hoping. Giving him one last chance. A single word would've sent her rushing into his arms. Just a single word.

Stay. That's all you have to say, Ben, she pleaded silently. *Stay.*

Pride alone kept him from reaching for her. *Go*, he thought. *Just get it the hell over with and go before I make an even bigger fool of myself!*

The doorbell rang as they stood there, a shrill sound that made Stacey jump even though she'd been expecting it. "That will be my taxi," she said. "No, don't bother to see me out," she added, though Ben had made no attempt to do so. She put her coffee cup down and picked up her two suitcases, turning to go, and then paused in the door for one last look.

Ben stood with his hands in the pockets of his robe, his bare ankles crossed as he leaned back against the counter. "Have a good trip," he said pleasantly, though it was killing him.

Stacey felt her heart begin to break. She stiffened her back. "You can have Marta send along what I've left behind," she said. "She has my address."

Ben straightened as the front door closed behind her. He drew his hands out of his pockets and deliberately, slowly, as if it pained him to do so, uncurled his clenched fists. He raised them to his face, pressing his thumbs into the throbbing, soul-deep ache behind his glittering eyes.

HER APARTMENT was exactly as she'd left it, though why she expected it to be any different she wasn't sure. She'd been gone less than a week, after all, and no one but the daily maid would have been in it during that time. Bernadine always left things exactly as she found them. But still, she'd expected it to be different, perhaps because she herself felt so different.

She unpacked her suitcases methodically, hanging what needed to be hung on padded, scented hangers in her huge walk-in closet, folding other things away in sachet-lined drawers, setting aside whatever needed to be cleaned or laundered for Bernadine to attend to. She was putting away her toiletries, fitting her perfumes and makeup neatly into their places on the bathroom shelves when she met her own eyes in the mirror. She paused in her task and flipped on the circle of makeup lights that surrounded it, leaning forward to study her reflection in the bright glare.

She'd changed, yes, but how? Her hand lifted, her fingers smoothing gently, curiously over her jawline and brow bones seeking...something. Her face was the same one that had stared back at her last week. The same clean jawline, the same fair creamy skin, the same pale pink lips and cheeks that always needed cosmetic help to keep her from looking like a porcelain doll, the same blue eyes.

Stacey stared into her eyes.

There was the change.

For all her adult life, she'd always been cool and rather remote looking. The image was partly the natural result of her pale hair and skin, partly a cultivated manner of reserve that had gradually become second nature. But her eyes she knew, because more than one person had told her, had always managed to hint at the real, warm woman beneath the image. Always before there'd been the hope, she realized, that one day she would go home to Iron Oakes—and to Ben. That hope was what had kept her warm and real for the past eleven years. It was what had saved her from becoming, in reality, the icy career woman she pretended to be. Now that hope was gone—forever—and her face showed it.

She felt as if all the warmth in her had gone up in flames, ignited by the blazing heat in Ben, and now that she'd moved away from his heat her own was gone, too, burned out with just the ashes left. Fine, cold ashes.

I should hate him for that, she thought, *but I can't. Somehow, I can't. He didn't ask Henry to make that will. If this whole, sorry mess is anybody's fault*, she thought, *it's Henry's*. But she couldn't find it in her heart to hate Henry, either. She couldn't find anything in her heart at all.

Shivering slightly, she switched off the glaring circle of makeup lights and quickly finished her unpacking, studiously avoiding looking into her own face.

She ran a bath then and, once dry, wrapped herself in another ivory silk nightgown and snuggled into the cashmere robe she'd thought of so longingly that morning at Iron Oakes. She wandered rather listlessly out into her tiny kitchen, intending to make herself some scrambled eggs and toast and a pot of good, strong coffee. She wasn't really hungry but it'd been hours since her last meal—at the Cipango with Ben—and she knew she should eat something. In the end, though, she ate only three or four bites of her makeshift meal and scraped the rest into the garbage. Leaving the dishes for Bernadine to do when she came in to clean in the morning, Stacey carried her coffee from the tiny kitchen, through the almost equally tiny but exquisitely chic dining room into the living room.

She set the cup and saucer down on a delicate end table and moved across the pale gray carpet to turn on the radio, selecting a soothing classical station as she did almost every night when she came home from work. Before sitting down she switched on the electric fire in the small fireplace with its white marble mantelpiece. She picked up her cup then, and tucked her bare feet up under her as she sipped her coffee and stared broodingly into the flames flickering over the fake logs, shivering slightly.

In less than a week she'd forgotten how cold it could get in Paris, even in the middle of July. Not that the fire offered any real warmth. One relied on the central heating for that and, because it was summer, the heat was, of course, turned off. She snuggled deeper into her cashmere robe, pulling the shawl collar up around her neck and tucked her feet farther under her. The coffee, her usual dark French roast, tasted weak and unappetizing, and the classical music playing softly on the radio failed to relax her. She put the cup aside and stood up, moving restlessly to the radio to change the station and then abruptly shut it off. She went to stand in front of the fire, her hands extended to the warmth.

She was cold, so cold, both inside and out, and the fire gave off only a feeble warmth. It wasn't enough to heat the coldness that seemed to surround her. She turned from it, her arms wrapped around her upper body in what was quickly becoming an habitual gesture and gazed around her living room. But even the sight of the beautifully decorated room failed to warm her. It was cold, too, she told herself, though it wasn't really true. Cold and formal and almost overpoweringly feminine.

Plush, pale gray carpet covered the living-room floor, giving way to the beautiful black-and-white marble squares of the dining room and the small foyer. The walls throughout were pale ice blue. The furniture was delicate and expensive, upholstered in pale shades of blue and gray silk brocade. Pale, pearl gray velvet drapes, pulled back over sheer white undercurtains, framed a lovely view of Paris's lights. There was an exquisite enameled clock centered on the white marble mantel with heavy silver candlesticks flanking it on either end.

It was apparent, Stacey realized for the first time, that no man shared the apartment with her and—she told herself inaccurately—apparent, too, that no man was welcome in this frigid bower of femininity. It seemed to her now to be cloyingly feminine. Perhaps that was why, she mused, she'd been so conscious of the overwhelming masculinity of Iron Oakes.

So be it, she thought, telling herself that she didn't care. The apartment was hers, a clear reflection and extension of her personality. She was now, in reality, cold and formal and icily feminine as opposed to what she had once been; hot-tempered and impetuous and warmly female. *Well, good*, she thought. It was safer that way.

She switched off the electric fire and went into her bedroom. The walls were pale blue in here, too, like the rest of the apartment. The carpet was a floral Aubusson in shades of blue and cream and pink. The bed was a huge gilt four poster dressed with pristine, frilly white linens and draped with white lace bed curtains lined with the palest pink silk she could find. It was a fantasy room fit for a princess. Each component, from the main pieces of furniture to the pink crystal perfume atomizers had been lovingly put together to make a pleasing whole.

Usually it brought a smile of satisfaction and contentment to her lips. Tonight she didn't even turn on a light to appreciate its beauty but instead just crawled into the bed, still wearing her robe, and pulled the comforter up over her head, seeking warmth.

SHE AWOKE EARLY, just as dawn was beginning to color the sky. Her arms were wrapped tightly around one of the pillows, and she was still burrowed like a small hurt animal under the lace-trimmed comforter.

And still cold. So cold.

She rose swiftly, scarcely glancing at the pink-tinged view of a slowly awakening Paris framed in her bedroom window, and quickly made herself ready for work. Showered, her pale face made up with warming colors of ivory foundation and peach-hued blusher, she dressed warmly in a long-sleeved, deep violet silk shirtwaist dress, matching pumps and a cream colored blazer. Automatically, practically without conscious thought, she accessorized her rather severe outfit with small gold hoops in her ears and a long gold chain looped twice around her neck to lie, softly gleaming, against the deep violet of her dress. A tiny lavender lace handkerchief peeked jauntily from the breast pocket of her blazer.

She had nearly three uninterrupted hours at the office before anyone else arrived, and she put it to good use, **reorganizing** the files that André's son, Edouard, had managed to reduce to inefficient chaos in the short time she'd been gone. She was just finishing up, on her knees before the lowest file drawer, when she heard the door open behind her.

"Stacey," exclaimed André in surprised delight. "You are back so soon! When you called, *mon Dieu*, it was only yesterday, was it not? I did not expect you back so soon. But I am pleased you are home, *chérie*. Very pleased." He came forward as he spoke, helping her to her feet, and then kissed her warmly on both cheeks. He held her away from him a little, still clasping her hands in both of his. "We have missed you very much. It is good to have you with us." He peered into her face with almost parental concern. "But perhaps you have come back too soon? You look a bit worn," he said worriedly. "You have had a long trip and a trying time, *oui*? Perhaps you should go home and rest for a few days. You look tired," he said, though tired wasn't exactly what he meant. He couldn't have put into words exactly what he meant. "As beautiful as ever, *chérie*, but tired."

Stacey laughed lightly, touched by his warm greeting. "I'm fine, André, really," she assured him, "and very eager to get back to work." She gently pulled her hands from his, "Let me get you your coffee, and perhaps a croissant to celebrate this prodigal's return? Do you know I haven't had a croissant since I left here? I'm dying for one," she said, moving toward the door. "Then you can fill me in on what progress has been made on the Jordan contract."

André nodded and let her go. When she returned with two coffees and the promised croissants they settled down to work, busy with all the things that hadn't been properly seen to by Edouard. In a very few minutes it was as if she'd never left. People popped in to say hello and welcome her back and express their belated condolences on the loss of her grandfather. Just before lunch, Edouard el-Hamid made a brief appearance. Seeing Stacey working busily at what had yesterday looked as if it was destined to be his desk, he hurried forward, kissing her hands in a lavish and theatrical display of gratitude for her return, and just as quickly hurried out again.

Things continued to be that way—busy—all the rest of the day. And the week. And the month. Stacey welcomed the frantic pace, seeing it as the perfect way to forget.

HER TWENTY-SEVENTH BIRTHDAY came and went. André bought her flowers to mark the occasion and took her to an extravagant lunch at her favorite little bistro. She received a loving, worried letter from Marta along with a trunk containing all of the clothes she'd left behind. But there was nothing from Ben.

Stacey shrugged and told herself that she didn't care and that it was better that way. Nothing was to be gained, she reasoned, from further contact with him. They had nothing to say to each other. Nothing at all.

She threw herself even more energetically into her work, telling herself daily that she was free of him now, finally, but she knew it was a lie. The cold she felt began to work itself deeper. Even when she accompanied André to Saudi Arabia to finalize the Jordan deal she felt the cold. It was becoming a part of her now, an accepted fact. In a way it was a good thing, she rationalized. It insulated her from feeling any pain and it made her a better employee to André because, she told herself, she had no emotional involvements to sidetrack her from the business at hand.

But André was becoming worried. "*Chérie*," he said to her one day near the Christmas holidays as he was preparing to leave for the afternoon, "why don't you take the rest of the afternoon off, too?" He waved a hand expressively. "Go shopping. Get your hair done. I give you leave."

Stacey looked up from her desk and smiled at him. "You just feel guilty for leaving early," she teased.

"*Non*, I do not. Well, perhaps, just a little but—" he smiled "—that is no reason for you not to take advantage of my guilt. Besides, when I am gone there is no work for you to do, *oui*?"

"When you are gone, André, is when I can get the most work done!" she informed him.

André shrugged dismissively. "Perhaps, but I am worried about you, *chérie*. You are working too hard, too much." He smiled at her faintly amused expression. "Yes, I know. I should be glad that you do since I benefit from your dedication. But you are a young, beautiful woman and I am a Frenchman before I am a businessman. I hate to see such a woman waste herself as you are doing. You should have a man. Someone special to spoil you." His Saudi accent was becoming more evident and Stacey was touched by his very real concern for her.

"What makes you think I don't?"

"*Mon Dieu!* Do not think you can pull so easily the sheep over my eyes! If you had a man he would not allow you to spend so many of your hours here when you could be spending them more pleasantly with him. *Non*, you cannot fool me! You have no special man, *chérie*."

"Oh, all right, André, I don't have a special man," she admitted laughingly. "But I'm a career girl, not a homemaker. I like my job and I like working for you," she assured him. "And besides, I see lots of men," she lied.

"Lots of men?" he echoed, unconvinced. "Who? When?"

"Tonight." She fabricated the when, adroitly skipping over the who part of his question. "I'm going to a Christmas party, and as soon as I finish proofing this report I'm going home to get ready."

"You are not pulling on my arm?" he said doubtfully.

"Leg," she corrected. "Pulling your leg. And no, I'm not, André." He still failed to look convinced. "Have I ever lied to you?" she asked.

André smiled then and chucked her under the chin. "Women always lie, *chérie*. They cannot help it." He laughed uproariously at her expression of mock outrage. "But come. Leave this report and I will drive you home."

"Remember," he said when he had dropped her in front of her apartment. "I will expect a detailed report on this party you are going to. And on this nonexistent man!"

Stacey actually did have a party she could go to—she hadn't lied to André about that. She had invitations to dozens of holiday parties, but she hadn't, until now, thought of going to any of them because she just wasn't in a party mood.

She kept thinking of Christmas in Texas, remembering the Mexican chocolate that Marta made for everyone to drink as they sat around the Christmas tree. They'd always had an old-fashioned tree decorated with red and green balls, strings of popcorn, tiny woven straw donkeys and angels and hammered metal stars and crosses that gave it a distinctly Southwestern flavor. She could see Marta's precious nativity scene set up on the mantel, its tiny figures carved of wood and painted by hand. The three kings all wore sombreros and serapes, as did the figure of Joseph. The gentle Mary's skirts were brightly hued, her braids long and black, partially cov-

ered by a white mantilla. Even the baby Jesus wore a
gaily striped serape as his swaddling clothes.

There'd always been a *piñata*, too, hung from the ceiling in the front hall and filled with small toys and hard
candies for all the ranch children, including Stacey, to try
to knock down, spilling its riches for everyone.

And the food! There would be rich fruitcake from
Corsicana, Texas—the only kind Marta would buy—
and homemade pralines, rich with caramel and pecans,
and Marta's special Mexican cinnamon cookies. For
Christmas dinner there would be Turkey *Mole*, a traditional festival dish reputed to have been invented by the
Mexican nuns at the convent of Santa Rosa in the six-
teenth century.

Marta used to tell the legend each year as Stacey stirred
the simmering *Mole*, redolent with tomatoes and on-
ions and garlic, plus almonds and raisins and sesame
seeds and always a bit of ground chocolate. A curious
hodgepodge of ingredients, to be sure, but her mouth
watered at the thought of the dish.

The thought of what she was missing at Iron Oakes,
seeing in her mind's eye all of her family sitting down to
Christmas dinner—without her—had made Stacey
apathetic and unenthusiastic toward any celebration of
the season. But, she thought now, perhaps André was
right.

Maybe she *was* wasting herself. There were dozens of
men, hundreds probably, who were capable of arousing
in her the same sort of response as Ben had done. Of
course there were, she told herself firmly. Ben wasn't the
only man in the world, not by a long shot. And just because she couldn't have an Iron Oakes' Christmas didn't
mean she should deny herself any celebration at all.

Stacey went to the party that night, and several others during the holiday season, up to and including the huge New Year's Eve bash that André always hosted. He was happy to see her there, apparently enjoying herself, and happier still when she allowed an attractive, unattached male to see her home. He wouldn't have been so happy to know that, after a chaste good-night kiss, the attractive man was sent on his way. Just as had several other men who had been allowed to escort her to and from some of the parties had been sent away. She just couldn't seem to take that final step and say the words that would invite them in.

Damn you, Ben, damn you to hell! she would think when the door closed on a mildly puzzled or sometimes downright angry escort of the evening. *That was a nice man*, she would tell herself after one of them had gone, *an attractive man, totally charming. And he leaves me cold.* And then she would undress and wrap herself in a nightgown and robe, crawling into bed with the covers pulled up over her head to dream, unwillingly, of Ben.

ALL TOO SOON January sped to a close and, with it, the will's six-month deadline approached and passed. The ranch was Ben's now, all Ben's. It was lost to her forever. She stayed home from work that day, locked in her apartment, and cried until her eyes were almost swollen shut and her pale complexion was blotched and red. This was the end of it then. It was no longer possible for her to change her mind.

Solemnly, she gathered up her mementos of Iron Oakes—her copy of Henry's will, some old photographs, the white lace mantilla Marta had given her—and switched on the electric fire in the fireplace. Ritualistically she began to burn them. First Henry's will, then the snapshots. But when it came time to consign Marta's gift to the flames she found that she couldn't do it. So she folded it away instead and hid it, out of sight, in a bottom drawer of her dresser.

EARLY IN FEBRUARY André made a request of her. "I must ask you to do something personal for me, *chérie*."

Stacey put aside the papers she was working on. "Yes, of course, André. What is it?"

"You will not be so eager when you hear what it is," he warned, then went on to explain. "My house, as you know, is still undergoing renovations."

Stacey smiled. Everyone in the building knew about André's house. A relatively small project to begin with, it had grown until nearly every room of what amounted to a small mansion was affected. André shouted daily at someone about his house, or had Stacey shout for him.

"I must entertain a client."

"Monsieur Verdant?" Stacey guessed correctly.

"*Oui*. Verdant," André nodded. "I cannot entertain him properly in my home and . . ." His voice trailed off suggestively.

"Would my apartment be big enough?" she offered, knowing very well what he was leading up to.

"It would be perfect!" André smiled with relief. "You are a treasure, *chérie*, a pearl without price!"

Stacey only smiled. "When is this little soirée to take place?" she asked, her pen held poised over the desk calendar to make a note of the date.

"Tonight."

"Tonight?" Stacey suppressed a sigh and looked up at him, the pen still in her hand. "That's not much notice, André," she reproved him gently, and he grinned rather sheepishly. "How many will there be?" she asked then, and they launched into a brief discussion of the particulars involved.

"Just cocktails," said André, "and some sort of hors d'oeuvres. I will leave that to you, *chérie*," he said, waving a hand in the air expressively. "We have tickets for the opera, you know."

Yes, she knew because she had made the reservations.

"So everything must run like a watch."

"Like clockwork," she corrected automatically. André looked at her quizzically. "Run like clockwork," she repeated.

"Watch, clockwork—" he shrugged "—it is all the same. Go, *chérie*, and see that it does."

"Is there anything special you'd like in the way of food?"

"I leave it entirely to you," he told her.

Stacey nodded, smiling indulgently, and went through to her own office. In less than ten minutes she had tidied up her desk and was ready to do André's bidding.

"I'll be gone for the rest of the day, Nicole," she said to her secretary as she paused to belt a street-length fur coat around her slender waist. She glanced at her watch, mentally juggling errands. "If Monsieur Verdant calls put him directly through to André, please. Anybody else, just take a message." She settled a fur beret jauntily on her head and pulled on dark leather gloves as she gave her instructions. "Let's see, did I leave anything out?"

"No, *mademoiselle*," said the secretary and then briefly repeated Stacey's instructions back to her.

"Good." Stacey smiled, her hand poised to push open the door. "Thank you, Nicole," she said and then stepped out into the cold winter air. She paused for a moment, turning up the collar of her coat against the chill and hailed a cab.

TWO HOURS LATER she made her precarious way to her building, laden with shopping bags and paper-wrapped flowers, the cabbie trailing along behind her with his arms full, too. She shouldered open the lobby door, pushed the elevator button with her elbow and then stood in front of her apartment door juggling packages and searching for her keys. She could feel the huge bouquet slipping from under her arm and she shifted it hurriedly, transferring the strap of her purse to her teeth as she did so.

"Here, let me take that for you," said a man's voice, speaking in English. A big, tanned hand reached out to take the purse and rescue the precariously held flowers.

Stacey's eyes flew up in stunned surprise, the automatic, "*Merci, monsieur,*" dying on her lips. "Ben," she mouthed soundlessly. "How...when..." But words failed her. She'd never expected to see him again, especially not here in Paris, at her apartment. She didn't know what to say, how to react.

"Hello, Stacey," he said in that deceptively lazy way of his.

"Hello, Ben," she managed then, her wits beginning to return. They stood gazing at each other for a breathless minute, both of them wondering what to say now that they'd said hello.

12

"MADEMOISELLE," said the cabbie on a plaintive note, breaking the spell that held them.

"Oh, *pardon, monsieur*. Ben, would you get those please?" she said, finally managing to dig out her keys and open the door. "You can put them right over there, on the sideboard." She turned to the cabbie, handing him his fare, *"Merci, monsieur,"* she dismissed him. The cabbie bowed slightly and left.

Stacey closed the door behind him and then took a deep, calming breath before turning around. "Well," she said and then hesitated. *What now?* she wondered. She couldn't ask him any of the things she really wanted to. *Do you lie awake nights, thinking and remembering, the way I do? Do you ache inside? Has your heart turned to ice?* No, she couldn't ask him those questions. "How are you, Ben?" she asked instead.

"I'm fine." He put his hands in his pockets to keep from reaching for her. "And you?"

"I'm fine, too." She gave a nervous laugh. "I'm fine, you're fine. We're both fine. Isn't that nice?" She realized suddenly that she was babbling. Her hands were clasped tightly in front of her. She dropped them to her sides. "I'm going to go take off my coat," she said. "The kitchen's that way, through the dining room. Make yourself a drink. I won't be a minute."

But she was considerably more than a minute.

She hurried to the relative sanctuary of her room and, once there, leaned for a moment against the closed door, her eyes shut tight against the vision of Ben standing on the black-and-white marble floor of her foyer.

Ben! Why was he here? What did he want? Why couldn't he just leave her alone? She'd almost—almost!—gotten over him, she lied to herself. She'd almost reached the point that she wasn't thinking about him every minute of every day. Oh, damn him, why was he here? And then, unbidden, unwelcome, came the thought, *I'm glad! Whatever the reason, I'm glad.*

The secret recesses of her heart conjured up the picture of him that her eyes had so recently seen. He looked so handsome, so big, standing there in her tiny foyer. He was so overwhelmingly the best of the quintessential American male in his jeans and cowboy boots and the heavy sheepskin-lined suede jacket with its furry collar turned up around his tanned face. The lights of the crystal chandelier glinted off his black hair and played up the tiny squint lines at the corners of his blue eyes. Just remembering how he'd looked made her knees weak.

She pushed herself away from the door and methodically removed her coat and hat, putting them away. She debated for a brief moment about changing her clothes and then decided against it. Her jade-green silk shirtwaist, accented by a heavy triple strand of pearls, was quite presentable—feminine and businesslike both. Besides, she'd only have to change again for André's cocktail party.

André's party! For a few minutes she'd completely forgotten about it. She made a quick telephone call to Bernadine, engaging her services for the evening, and then hurried to the bathroom to smooth her hair and check her makeup. It was perfect, as usual, and not a hair was out of place. She turned on the taps, running cold water over the throbbing pulses in her wrists in an unconscious effort to cool her suddenly too-warm self. She realized then, with a small shock of surprise, that for the first time in months she wasn't cold.

Her eyes went to the mirror. Her cheeks were faintly flushed, her eyes were bright with...what? Anticipation? Excitement? Fear? Or a little of all three, perhaps? She didn't know, and she told herself very firmly, she didn't want to know. She turned off the taps, dried her hands and went determinedly out into the kitchen.

Ben had made himself a drink as she'd suggested, apparently having had no trouble finding the bourbon and the bar glasses. He'd taken off his sheepskin jacket, which was draped casually over the back of a kitchen chair, and was busy unpacking her groceries. He looked huge—he *was* huge—moving around in her small kitchen.

She stood watching him for a few seconds, admiring the fit of the soft white turtleneck sweater he wore and the way it stretched across the muscles of his back as he put away the pâtés and cheeses and fitted the bottles of wine into her small refrigerator.

"You always seem to be shopping," he said, startling her. She hadn't realized he was aware of her presence behind him. "First it was clothes, now food." He glanced over his shoulder, his grin intended to take the sting out of his words. "Good thing you're a rich bitch, the way you like to spend money," he teased. He thought maybe he should have kept his feeble jokes to himself when she frowned.

"Not my money," she said, coming into the room to help him. "André's money. It's his party."

Ben's face changed suddenly and the grin faded. He turned away from her. "How is André?" he asked tightly.

Now what brought that on? she wondered. And then she remembered. Ben thought André was her lover, because she'd wanted him to think that. Well, she still wanted him to think that. It was better that way, infinitely better. "André is exceedingly fine," she said.

Ben nodded shortly and turned back to the grocery sack.

She stared at him for a few seconds, wondering where to begin, what questions to ask. Because there *were* questions to be asked. He hadn't come to Paris on a whim. "Why are you here, Ben?"

He turned to her, resting his lean hips back against the kitchen counter, and folded his arms across his broad chest. "It's about Henry's will," he said, watching her for a reaction. He didn't know what he expected, nor even quite what he wanted. But whatever it was, it *wasn't* the quick frown that creased her brows.

"Henry's will? I thought we'd settled that." She stared up at him, puzzled and strangely excited. "Iron Oakes is yours." Her eyes fell and then fluttered upward again. "Isn't it?"

He shook his head. "Not entirely."

"Not entirely?" Stacey echoed faintly. Her voice shook. What did he mean, *Not entirely?*

"There are some final papers for you to sign."

"Papers?" she said. What papers? And why couldn't he have just mailed them? Why come all the way to Paris? There had to be more to it than that.

"Mademoiselle" came a voice from the direction of the foyer, "it is I, Bernadine."

"In here, Bernadine," Stacey called, her eyes still holding Ben's. "We're in the kitchen."

An older woman, gray haired and comfortably plump in a plain black dress, joined them in the kitchen. *"Bon-*

jour, mademoiselle," she said, and then her eyes flickered to Ben. They widened with a true Frenchwoman's appreciation for a superb male specimen.

"Bernadine, this is—" Stacey paused only half a second "—my uncle from America, Ben Oakes. Ben this is Madame Bernadine Bonnard. She's going to help with the party tonight."

"Your uncle, *mademoiselle?"* Bernadine asked in French, not sure she'd heard right.

"Yes, my uncle," Stacey said firmly.

Bernadine shrugged expressively as if to say that she didn't really believe Stacey, but if that's what she wanted to pretend then she, Bernadine, would go along with it. *"Bonjour,* Monsieur Oakes," she said, inclining her head.

"Pleased to meet you, ma'am," Ben replied easily.

"Come on, Uncle Ben," said Stacey. "Let's get out of the kitchen and let Bernadine get to it."

Ben smiled a farewell at the maid and picked up his sheepskin jacket, following Stacey out of the kitchen.

"Where are you going?" she demanded as he continued on toward the front door.

"To my hotel."

"You can't drop a bombshell like that and then just leave—"

"Look, Stacey," he interrupted, "obviously you're having a party tonight and this is something we need to talk about without interruptions. It's not exactly party chatter. I'll come back tomorrow." He shrugged into his jacket, moving toward the door.

"Wait!" she commanded as his hand reached for the door knob. "Come back tonight."

He looked at her questioningly from under lowered lids.

"It's a cocktail party and everyone will be leaving for the opera at eight-thirty," she explained.

"Not you?"

She shook her head. "*Flying Dutchman* tonight. I don't appreciate Wagner." She reached for his coat sleeve. "Come back at, oh, quarter to nine. Everyone will be gone then. We can talk about—" a tiny pause "—about Henry's will."

He nodded, but for some reason she wasn't appeased.

Her fingers tightened on his sleeve. "Promise you'll come back," she demanded, needing to hear him say he would.

"I promise," he said softly, staring down into her upraised face. It was the face that had haunted his dreams for months now. Fine-boned, fragile yet strong, beautiful. Quickly, before he could tell himself not to, he raised his hands, cupping her face, and touched his lips to hers. It was just a brief kiss, one that even Bernadine would have thought entirely appropriate between an uncle and niece had she happened to see it. But its briefness wasn't the whole story.

In that scant second that his lips claimed hers, Stacey felt herself suffused with warmth as a most unniecely heat flooded her body. Ben felt like a starving man who'd been granted a small taste of ambrosia. He sighed softly—a sigh that was echoed by Stacey—and his hands fell from her face.

"See you later, honey," he said, his voice sounding unnaturally rough to his own ears.

Stacey stood for a few short moments, trembling a little, one hand raised wonderingly to her lips as she stared at the closed door.

Why had he kissed her, she wondered vaguely and then, why, oh why, had she made him promise to come back later, when everyone would be gone and she would be alone? Stupid, she berated herself. And yet, at the same time, she couldn't completely ignore that rebellious part of her that was eagerly anticipating his return.

Call his hotel and cancel, her mind urged her, *tell him you've changed your mind. That you're going to the opera, after all.* But which hotel? She didn't know, did she? So she couldn't call, could she? Of course not! She turned back toward the kitchen, conveniently forgetting that a few telephone calls to some of the best hotels in Paris would easily reveal his whereabouts.

"There will be seven for cocktails, Bernadine, including myself," she said, giving the maid a few last minute instructions. "All of the guests will be leaving promptly at eight-thirty so it won't be a late evening for you. Monsieur el-Hamid has seats for the opera," she explained. "You can set everything up buffet style in the dining room, okay? Oh, and use the big blue glass bowl for the flowers."

"Oui, mademoiselle, très bien," Bernadine answered placidly, already pulling platters and serving trays from their places.

Stacey went to her room then, confident that everything was well under control in Bernadine's capable hands, and began to ready herself for the evening ahead.

She lingered in her bath, reveling in the warmth and fragrance, and then dried herself lingeringly, smoothing on Opium lotion, dusting scented powder over her satiny legs and arms and flat belly.

She wandered back and forth between her bathroom and bedroom; fixing her hair, applying a heavier, more glamorous evening makeup with deep, smokey shadow emphasizing her blue eyes and clear red lipstick that made her skin seem even more porcelain pale by contrast. She began to dress then, when she was satisfied that her face and hair were as perfect as she could make them.

She slipped into her undergarments—a frilly little garter belt made mostly of black lace, a pair of high-cut tap pants and a strapless bra the color of coffee with lots of cream, also liberally frosted with black lace. Sitting on the velvet covered stool in front of her dressing table, she smoothed fine black stockings up her legs, fastening them to the garters. Then she stood up, ready for the dress.

She'd known since the door closed behind Ben that she was going to wear it. She'd bought it on a whim because she'd fallen in love with it at first sight. Now she knew that she had purchased it for just such an occasion as this, when she would need all the self-confidence that such a dress could give her. She lifted it off its padded hanger and slipped into it. It settled around her like a sigh, soft and shimmery.

The season's latest "little black dress," done this year in tissue-thin, gleaming panne velvet, irresistibly ornamented with a thin braid of gold silk cord along the wide bandeau neck and at the seams of the dropped shoulders. The narrow, chemise style just skimmed over her full breasts and slender hips, hinting at the body beneath it. It stopped two inches above her knees.

She stepped into plain black satin pumps with three-inch heels and tiny gold bows on the toes, fastened sparkling gold-and-diamond drops in her ears and then added one more perfect jewel, a gold butterfly with diamond-tipped feelers in the coil of her upswept hair. She stood back and smiled at the coolly elegant, leggy creature in the mirror. She was ready now. Ready for anything—or anyone.

She left the bedroom, hoping it was true.

"Ah, *mademoiselle!*" exclaimed Bernadine as Stacey appeared in the kitchen to check on the progress of the party preparation. "You look *superbe!*" she said effusively.

"Thank you, Bernadine. How are things going in here?"

"All is in readiness," Bernadine replied, motioning toward the dining room table. "All that is needed now are your guests, *n'est-ce pas?*"

"The table is beautiful, Bernadine. Simply beautiful."

And indeed it was. The pâtés rested atop white paper-lace doilies on silver trays, the cheeses were displayed on a bed of tender green ferns, the bite-size crepes were kept warm in a silver chafing pan, the luscious golden pears and red apples were mounded in a big crystal bowl to show them off to best advantage, the breads and assorted crackers were piled into silver gilt baskets lined with blue linens. All of it was artistically and efficiently arranged on the oval cherrywood table with a stack of pure white china plates, two rows of sparkling crystal wine glasses, a spray of gleaming cutlery and, in the center, a truly magnificent arrangement of white roses and baby's breath in a blue glass bowl.

Satisfied that everything was perfect in the dining room, Stacey wandered into the living room and prowled nervously around, twitching a table skirt here, adjusting a pillow there, turning off one lamp and switching on another, opening the drapes to their fullest to take advantage of her really rather spectacular view of the City of Light. The doorbell chimed, its three-toned bell echoing throughout the apartment. Stacey heard Bernadine's unhurried footsteps on the marble tiles as she moved to open the door and then, a second later, the distinctively accented rumble of André's voice.

She let out her breath, unaware until this minute that she'd been holding it, realizing that she'd been unconsciously poised, tensed, to hear Ben's deep, lazy drawl. Somehow, for some unexplainable reason, she thought he'd come back early and crash the party...or something.

Some part of her, also for some unexplainable—or unacknowledgeable—reason had halfway wanted him to. Because somewhere, deep in the most feminine recesses of her being, she'd wanted the chance to show him off to her Paris friends, just once, even if it was only as her uncle.

She went forward to greet her guests, a warm smile of welcome on her lips. "Come in," she said warmly, holding out both her hands to André.

"Ah, Stacey, *chérie*, how beautiful you look!" He kissed her on both cheeks, then leaned back to look at her again. *"Exquise!"* he said and kissed her cheeks a second time.

"Thank you, André," she returned his salute in like manner and then turned to hold out a graceful hand to Monsieur Verdant. *"Bienvenue!"* she said, welcoming him. Bernadine came forward to take their coats as introductions were made all around.

Stacey shook hands with Madame Verdant, an elegant woman dressed in a brown velvet Chanel evening suit with a big-collared gold tissue blouse, and Mademoiselle Verdant, a bright-eyed girl of about eighteen in the latest bit of bright nonsense of Zandra Rhodes and impossibly red hair that was only just saved from being punk by the way it curled on her neck and forehead.

"Call me Rivi," she said, ignoring the quelling glance of her mother. "Mademoiselle Verdant sounds so stuffy." She shrugged expressively, her shining copper-colored lips pursing distastefully and then she smiled again. "Hey, I like your dress!"

Stacey smiled, thanking her, and turned to her last two guests, Monsieur and Madame Carpentier, other business associates of André's. She extended her hand graciously and her smile froze.

Ben had come early after all. He stood just behind the Carpentiers, smiling lazily at her over their heads, looking very pleased with himself and very handsome and elegant in a black tuxedo.

"Magnifique!" Rivi whispered sotto voce, her bright eyes round with admiration. "That man, he is something serious, *oui*?" she said to no one in particular and grinned in open and very youthful provocation at the object of her admiration.

Stacey recovered herself quickly, thankful that although Ben might have understood—no, definitely understood from the look in his eyes—the first word of Rivi's praise he couldn't have understood it all.

"Do come in, Ben," she managed to say with commendable calm, despite the excited fluttering of her pulse. "I'd like you to meet the rest of my guests. This is Ben Oakes, everyone, my un—a relative from America," she said and introduced everyone in turn.

"And this," she said, tucking a hand in André's elbow and drawing him forward, "is André, my boss and very good friend." She smiled at André, putting a subtle emphasis on the word "friend." "Isn't that so, André?"

"Oui," agreed André, smiling back at her. He looked at Ben. "So you are Ben Oakes," he said consideringly in English, a little hardness creeping into his voice. "The

man who has caused our Stacey so much—" he paused "—annoyance."

Stacey's eyes flew to Ben's face to see how he would take that. He smiled a hard-edged, dangerous smile.

"The very one," he agreed quite pleasantly except for the gleam in his eyes, "and likely to cause her even more—" he paused infinitesimally as André had done "—annoyance in the future."

Their eyes held for the briefest of moments, like two challenging male animals, intent on sizing each other up.

So this is Stacey's lover, Ben thought. He was a little old for her and not very loverlike in his attitude toward her. In fact, Ben decided, if she hadn't already told him about it, he'd have never guessed at the relationship between them. *If*, he thought suddenly, *there was a relationship—that kind of relationship—between them.*

André smiled then, a small smile of satisfaction, and he nodded once. *"Bien,"* he said and extended his hand.

The hardness went out of Ben's eyes as he reached out to meet it. "Glad to make your acquaintance at last," he said. They shook, very much as if a silent deal had just been most agreeably concluded.

Stacey's eyes flickered back and forth between them, wondering what had just happened. It seemed as if they liked and even understood each other. And yet nothing had been said and only that very brief, almost hostile, look had passed between them before they shook hands.

She shrugged, a tiny, uneasy movement of her shoulders. "Let's all go into the living room, shall we?" she invited. She made a slight movement with her hand, unseen by anyone but Bernadine, who followed them into the softly lit gray-and-blue room with a tray of glasses and wine bottles in a silver cooler.

Comfortably settled, drinks in hand they began to converse about the usual things that people who don't really know each other well talk about: movies, books, the opera to be seen that night. Stacey noticed, without seeming to, that Ben and young Rivi Verdant weren't participating in the general conversation. Sitting side by side in a corner of the sofa, they were carrying on a semiprivate conversation of their own.

"I just love Americans!" Rivi was saying in delightfully accented English. "They are so different," she went on, her lashes fluttering up and down flirtatiously, blatantly inviting Ben to flirt back. "Are all Americans as big as you?" she asked.

"Only the ones from Texas," Ben drawled.

"Tex-sas," Rivi cooed. "Tell me about Tex-sas, *s'il vous plaît*. I have seen it on the television, oh, many times. Tell me about J.R. Is he really so mean?"

Stacey turned away, a delicate sneer on her lips as she tuned out his explanation about how the fictional J. R. Ewing and the rest of the Ewing clan as seen on the television series "Dallas" had no bearing on reality.

Jealousy stabbed at her vitals and she clenched her fingers around the champagne flute in her hand, appalled that she responded so . . . so viscerally to something that was really so basically innocent. After all, she told herself, Rivi might be flirting for all she was worth, but the only reaction she was getting from Ben was one of amused indulgence. And yet, it was all she could do not to leap across the room and scratch the eyes out of Mademoiselle Rivi's harmless, empty little head.

André made a comment then, about the time, and everyone rose, en masse, and wandered toward the dining room to sample the delicacies that had been prepared for them.

"I just love champagne!" Rivi sparkled up at Ben. "It so tickles my nose."

"Tell me," said André a few minutes later as he drew Ben into conversation. "What is it that you do in Texas?"

Stacey watched with growing apprehension as they talked, too far away for her to be able to hear what was said, too friendly for her to fool herself into thinking that they were acting like rivals for her favors.

And then, suddenly, it was time to leave for the opera. There was a flurry of fur coats and cheek kissing and André whispered in her ear. "I like your Ben," he said. "Mademoiselle Rivi was quite right. He is something very serious."

"He's not my Ben," Stacey started to protest, but André only smiled and put a finger to her lips, silencing her. And then he turned and shepherded his guests out the door.

Stacey stood for a moment, her hand on the doorknob, gathering the courage to go back into the living room and face Ben. The time had come to find out why he'd traveled all the way to Paris. She couldn't really believe it was just to get her to sign some papers, whatever they were. There had to be more to it than that. But she had no idea what it could possibly be. Well, she decided, whatever it was, she wanted it over as quickly as possible.

13

Ben was waiting for her when she returned to the living room. He'd removed his tuxedo jacket. Stacey could see it crumpled on the floor behind him, obviously fallen from the back of the chair where he'd carelessly flung it. His bow tie was undone, hanging loose around his neck, and the top few buttons of his pleated white dress shirt were unbuttoned. The pleats—narrow, discreet, stylish—seemed to emphasize the rampant masculinity of their wearer.

And how well he knows it, thought Stacey, forgetting or ignoring the fact that her own dress emphasized what was most female about her.

He extended a brimming tulip-shaped champagne glass toward her. "Come and sit down," he said easily when she took it. "Bernadine's fixed us a big plate of everything." He motioned toward the plate on the coffee table, laden with slices of cheese and pâté, wedges of ripe fruit and rounds of bread spread thickly with fresh, yellow butter.

Sitting, Stacey set her champagne flute on the coffee table and reached for the plate, layering a slice of rich pâté on a piece of buttered bread. She bit into it hungrily. "How did you ask her to do this?" she asked. "She speaks very little English and I know you don't speak French. Do you?" she tacked on suspiciously.

He shook his head. "I didn't have to ask," he said, spreading Camembert on a wedge of sweet, juicy pear.

He grinned. "I guess I just looked hungry. Your Bernadine is a lot like Marta, always trying to feed somebody."

"How is Marta?" Stacey asked softly.

"She's fine." Ben bit into his pear and paused, swallowing. "Misses you a lot. She was hurt that you didn't say goodbye," he said carefully, watching Stacey. She'd been good and angry, too, accusing Ben of driving her precious *niña* away.

Stacey reached for her champagne glass just to have something to do. "I wrote to her and explained."

"Um-hmm," he said, his mouth full of food. "Explained what?"

Stacey's head came up at his tone. "Why I left, of course. What else would I explain? I said I loved her and would miss her, but that I just couldn't see myself living at Iron Oakes anymore." Her voice began to shake a little. Why was Ben questioning her like this? It was a sure bet that he'd seen her letter to Marta, so why this cross-examination? "I said that my life was here now and—"

"Did you tell her about André? That you were coming back to be with your lover?" He knew, now, that André wasn't her lover and never had been. She'd lied to him about that. It made him wonder what else she'd lied to him about.

"Well, not in those exact words," Stacey said. "But, yes, I told her about André." She paused and then looked up at him, defiance in her eyes as she stared into his. "Why are we going over this?" she asked, almost pleadingly. "I'm sure Marta showed you the letter. She always does. You already know what I told her."

Ben nodded. "But you lied," he said, pinning her into the corner of the sofa with the look in his eyes, laser hot as they bored into her. "And I'm just beginning to realize it."

"Lied?" she said indignantly, trying to quell him with an imperious lift of her head.

"Lied," he said flatly, inordinately pleased by the fact. He didn't usually like being lied to, but in this instance, it thrilled him. "André is no more your lover than Uncle Pete is," he stated matter-of-factly. "He's your boss and your good friend, like you said, but that's all."

"That's all *now*," she lied again, looking down into the champagne glass in her hand. She twisted it by the stem. She didn't know why all this seemed to be so important to him, why he even cared what her relationship with André was or was not. It didn't matter now. Iron Oakes was his.

"Not entirely." The words echoed in her mind, warning her of some unknown danger. Why not entirely? Why not . . . but the thought slipped away as she looked up and encountered the burning heat in his eyes.

He still wanted her, she realized, a shock of something like high-voltage electricity tingling along her nerve endings. Had he really come all this way just because he still wanted her, she wondered incredulously. And did he really think she'd fall into his arms because he had?

"The affair was over a few months ago," she said with a careless shrug, trying desperately to keep herself from doing just that. Because, heaven help her, she still wanted him, too. Wanted him with an intensity and a fire that had not, after all, turned to cold ashes. It had merely been banked somewhere deep within her and was now, ignited by his presence, threatening to explode and burn out of control. If he touched her, if she allowed him to reach her in any way, the flames would consume her completely. "And you know me. Off with the old, on with the new."

"Who?" he asked.

"What does it matter who?" She shifted away from him, reaching out to set her untouched champagne on the coffee table. "Besides, it's none of your business."

He reached and captured her hand. "I think you're lying again," he said softly.

She jerked her hand away, frightened by what his slightest touch did to her already churning insides, and stood up, moving out of his reach. "I don't care what you think," she said tersely, her back to him.

She heard him move, felt his hand on her shoulder and she whirled out of his reach again, facing him. "Don't touch me," she warned softly and then, "Oh, why don't you go back to the ranch where you belong and leave me alone! Just go home."

He reached out and grasped her shoulders, forcing her to stand still and face him. "Home?" he queried, encouraged by her unthinking reference to Iron Oakes as home. "Isn't this your home?"

No, she wanted to say, to scream. *No this isn't my home.* But she didn't. "You're hurting me," she said calmly.

His face paled at her softly spoken words, and a taut, strained line twisted his mouth in a self-directed grimace of disgust. "I'm sorry," he said, loosening his hold on her. "I always seem to be hurting you, one way or another."

"*Pardon, mademoiselle,*" said Bernadine hesitantly from the doorway. "I am ready to leave now. Is there anything further you or the *monsieur* wish before I go?"

"No nothing, thank you, Bernadine," she said, speaking in French as the maid had done. "You did a lovely job with the table. The flowers were beautiful."

"*Merci, mademoiselle*. If that is all then, *bonne nuit*."
She turned to go and then stopped short, catching sight
of Ben's dinner jacket where it lay in a crumpled heap on
the floor. Tsking softly, she moved forward to pick it up.
As she did so something shiny fell out of one of the
pockets. She stooped to pick it up. "*Mademoiselle*, it is
the cigarette case you thought you had lost!" She crossed
the room to hand it to Stacey. "How considerate of the
handsome *monsieur* to bring it for you from America,
n'est-ce pas?"

"Yes, very considerate," acknowledged Stacey softly.

There was a small, tense silence after Bernadine had
gone. Stacey stood staring down at the cigarette case,
turning it over and over in her slim fingers. "Where did
you find it?" she said at last, her eyes still fixed on the gold
case in her hands.

"On the table where you left it that first day."

Her eyes flew up to his, wide and questioning. "You
had it all this time?"

He nodded slowly, holding her eyes with his, careful
not to touch her in any other way. "It was in my breast
pocket at the Cipango," he admitted. "I could have given
it to you then, when you wanted a cigarette, but—" He
lifted his big shoulders in a shrug, looking not the least
bit French as he did it but totally, thoroughly American
and male and very, very dear to her.

"Why?" she said softly, almost on a whisper as something fluttered in the region of her heart.

"It reminded me of you," he said and his hand reached
out to her, softly touching her cheek in a brief, careful
caress. "Slim and elegant and cool." His hand dropped.
"I wanted something of you."

"I don't understand, Ben," she said, but she thought
she was beginning to, a little. Maybe. Tentative hope

surged through her. "Why would you want something of mine?"

He looked at her for a long, silent minute, debating his answer. A lie would be a sop to his pride, already bruised by chasing her to Paris and not having her fall into his arms on sight. The truth would get everything out in the open at last. It might also make him more miserable. But, hell, he thought, pride had already made him as miserable as he ever wanted to be. "Because I love you," he said, abruptly deciding to tell the truth. He had to say it to her, at least once.

"You love me?" she echoed, scarcely daring to believe that she'd heard him right. The wild fluttering of her heart became a hammer in her chest, threatening to choke off her breath. She stood silently, staring at him with wide, startled eyes.

He took her silence for disbelief or perhaps disgust. Turning away from her, he ran a hand through his black hair. "I've loved you since you were just a kid," he admitted raggedly, determined to lay it all out on the table now that he'd started. "Like a sister at first. The sweet, adoring little sister that I never had, offering the unconditional love that no one had ever given me before. And then, that summer I graduated from Tech and came back to Iron Oakes for good, you'd changed. My little sister was gone...changed into a woman, and I couldn't make myself see you as a sister anymore. How I wanted you then! And how I hated myself for wanting you!" he grated through clenched teeth. "A little girl of fifteen and I could barely keep my hands off you!"

"I wanted you, too," Stacey said to his back.

"You only thought you did, which made it all the worse, all the harder for me to resist." He turned to look down into her face and his gaze was fiercely tender. "You weren't old enough to know what you wanted," he explained as his eyes roamed hungrily over her upraised face. "You were just a half-grown kid, eager to know what life was all about. Any man would have done." His hands clenched, the knuckles showing white. "And I couldn't stand that, either! That's why I got you sent away, you know, I couldn't—wouldn't—let myself be the one and I couldn't bear to stand by and watch it be somebody else."

"No," she breathed, her eyes reading and returning the hunger in his. "There was never anyone else, Ben. It was only you, then."

"And now?" he asked very, very softly. He felt as if his whole life depended on her answer.

Stacey scarcely paused to think about what she was saying. She, too, had had enough of false pride. It was a cold companion, and a poor substitute for the love she wanted and needed. "It's always been you," she answered him, her heart in her eyes. "All my life it's been you. Even those eleven years when I . . . when I thought you didn't want me and I tried to hate you for it, it was still you, Ben." Her hands fluttered up between them. "I can't seem to help it."

He reached for her hands, pulling her to him gently, carefully, and she heard him sigh, a deep, ragged sound, as his arms folded her to him. They stood like that for a few, endless minutes, holding each other close, her head against the muscled wall of his chest, his cheek against her hair. They were content, for the moment, just to hold each other.

In a little while, though, contentment alone wasn't enough. She felt his lips against the top of her head and his hands on her back began to move in small, caressing circles. She pulled a little away from his gentle embrace to look up into his face.

"Make love to me, Ben," she said softly. "Please. Before I die from wanting you."

She saw the flare of hungry passion in his face and, more importantly, the love that was shining in his eyes, as he silently bent and lifted her in his arms. Her own curled around his neck.

"Which way?" he asked hoarsely. Silently, she pointed the way to her bedroom.

He set her on her feet by the big four-poster bed, letting her body slide slowly down the hard length of his as he did so. His hands came up and slowly, carefully, his eyes never leaving her face, he took the gold butterfly from her hair and laid it on her bedside table. Then, one by one, he removed the pins that held the heavy blond coil in place. When all the pins were out, scattered carelessly on the carpet, he combed his hands sensuously through the golden curtain of her hair, loosening and fluffing it around her face.

"Wildcat," he growled, low, his hands on either side of her face. "My wildcat."

"Yes," Stacey breathed, turning her lips into his hand as instinct had so often urged her to do. Her tongue came out to seductively tickle his palm. Ben groaned and his hands fell to her shoulders.

"How does this thing come off?" he demanded, a ragged note of impatient passion in his voice. He struggled to control it.

"Over my head," she instructed, raising her arms. "Just pull."

She stood docilely as he carefully pulled the velvet dress off over her head, watching in fascination as his eyes widened appreciatively and then narrowed in helpless desire as he devoured her scantily clad form. She was barely covered by the silk and lace of her wickedly sexy, seductively female undergarments. He looked around for somewhere to lay the fragile dress, but Stacey reached out, taking it from him, and dropped it carelessly to the floor.

And then she became the aggressor. Her slender fingers slowly unbuttoned his cuffs and then removed the studs from the front of his shirt, pressing tiny, teasing kisses along his furred chest as each new bit of skin was revealed. She pulled the shirttail from the waistband of his slacks and, boldly holding his eyes, lowered her hand to the buckle of his belt.

"Stacey," he breathed raggedly, pushed to his limit by her frank desire. "Stacey, honey, slow down." He reached for her hands, pulling them away from his starving body. He meant to go slowly this time. To love her slowly and tenderly, with the exquisite care she deserved.

But Stacey wouldn't let him. She pressed up against him, going up on tiptoe, and fused their mouths together. They clung—hot, wet and so very hungry for each other. Their tongues came seeking each other's sweetness, their teeth nibbled at each other's lips, their heads turned and twisted, searching out new angles, new pressures, new pleasures. Ben let go of her hands to wrap his arms around her pliant, willing body. Her hands went immediately to his belt buckle.

"Please," she whispered into his mouth. "Please, Ben." She lowered her hand a bit, touching him through the fabric of his slacks, and curled her fingers around the length and hardness of him. "I need you so much."

Ben moaned and pulled her down onto the bed. They feasted on each other—touching and stroking all the sweet, hidden places, their mouths still feeding passionately on the other as if neither could ever get enough. Ben broke away, finally, one hand coming up to curve against her cheek.

"This is just us," he said intently, staring into her eyes. "No memories of some other night. No crazy will, pushing us at each other. Just you and me. Here and now."

"Just us," she murmured. "Just us." Just the two of them, following the dictates of their yearning hearts.

He unhooked her bra, tossing it to the floor, and tenderly covered her bared breast with his right hand. "Tell me if I hurt you, honey," he said against her neck. "I don't want to hurt you, ever again."

"You can't hurt me, Ben. Not now," she said, meaning emotional, not physical, hurt. As far as she was concerned, he'd never hurt her physically. He didn't have it in him to hurt her physically. She touched his cheek, arching her back as she guided his mouth to her breast. "Not when I know you love me."

But he was determined to handle her gently just the same. Obeying her silent directions, he slid down her body and took her nipple into his mouth. Slowly, tenderly, he sucked on her, teasing the hardened peak until she was writhing beneath him. He ran his hand down her torso to where the white satin skin of her thigh was exposed between the hem of the lace-covered tap pants and the top of her stockings. Unerringly, his fingers slid up under the wide-legged panties, honing in on the shadowed delta between her legs.

She stiffened and arched higher, pushing her breast into his mouth. One hand clutched at his hair. "Oh, yes, Ben. Yes. Please," she murmured frantically. Her legs opened wider, the moist feminine core of her needing his touch, all of her eager for the completion of his love. Her hands urged him to cover her body with the weight and strength of his.

"Slow down, honey," he whispered, trying to hold himself back. His hand retreated to her thigh in an effort to cool both of them down. "Take it easy."

"No," she pouted. "I don't want to take it easy. I want you to take me." She ran her hands down the front of his body and opened the fly of his pants. "Now," she demanded, slipping her hand inside to caress him.

Ben groaned and fell back against the bed, helpless as a child under her caressing hands. "Stacey, honey, please . . ." He didn't know if he was begging her to stop or to go on.

But Stacey knew. She lifted her hips off the bed, sliding off her underpants so that she was clad in only her lacy black garter belt and stockings. Then she rose up on her knees and began to undress him.

She was beautiful, he thought, gazing up at her through passion-drugged eyes. She was female incarnate—feral, deliciously wanton, hungry, wanting, giving. Her face was flushed and eager, her eyes glowing, her lips parted and gleaming in the dim light streaming in through the open bedroom door. Her hair was in wild disarray. Her breasts were full and creamy, thrusting toward him, the pink nipples hard and pointed with desire. Her slim waist flowed into the alluring, palm-pleasing curve of her hips. The soft downy triangle of blond hair between her thighs was enticingly, excitingly, lasciviously framed by the black lace of her garter belt. Her long slim legs were encased in fantasy-inspiring sheer black stockings.

"Stacey, honey," he moaned again. He lay flat on his back in her frilly, feminine bed, his once pristine dress shirt off one arm and wrinkled under him, his pants down around his thighs. "You're killing me."

She lifted her head, her hands stilling against his engorged body. "Do you want me to stop?"

"No! No," he breathed. "I may be dying of pleasure, but I'm not crazy." He groaned as her hands continued their fevered caresses. "Not yet."

"You will be," she promised, stroking him. "We both will."

He reached for her then, his big hands closing over the curve of her hips. "Let's go crazy together," he whispered raggedly, lifting her over him.

Stacey complied eagerly. Swinging one leg across his supine body, she balanced one hand on his damp chest and reached between them to position him. She gasped when he entered her that first tiny bit, her body tensing in anticipation of the pleasure to come. She stilled, savoring the feeling for just a moment. Impatiently, Ben's hands tightened on her hips, and he pulled her down, hard, burying himself to the hilt in her moist receptive warmth. She cried out, nearly screaming his name with the intensity of the feelings that filled her.

He went stiff beneath her. "Stacey?" Had he hurt her again? Had he—?

But she was moving on him, rocking above him in mounting ecstasy. "Ben-Ben-Ben-Ben," she chanted. "Love me. Love me."

He hadn't hurt her, but still, he hesitated. Their first coupling had been so frenzied, so rushed and primitive, that he'd wanted this time to be different. He'd wanted to go slowly with her, to show her how much he loved her. He wanted to take the time to cherish her body and to show her he could be gentle. But she obviously didn't want that. And, truthfully, neither did he. There would be plenty of time for gentleness later. They had a whole lifetime of "laters" now.

He tightened his hands on her gyrating hips, his biceps bunching and coiling as he helped her lift and lower herself above him. Their bodies pulled tighter, straining toward each other, striving to give the ultimate pleasure to each other while taking it for themselves.

Stacey peaked first. Her body tensed into one long line, her spine arching, her head falling back as completion took her. Ben uttered a triumphant shout and let go of her hips to push himself upright. His arms went around her back, holding her quivering body tight. He took her mouth in a searing kiss and exploded into an ecstasy of his own.

They floated back down to the bed in a cloud of sensual, loving feelings, arms locked around each other, pressing kisses against cheeks and chins and foreheads. Two pairs of eyes gazed at each other, glazed with emotional tears and the satisfaction of a long-denied passion, finally fulfilled. Two pairs of lips smiled and whispered loving endearments. Two souls joined, exalting in contentment and joy and love. Two exhausted bodies snuggled underneath the rose-strewn comforter and fell asleep.

STACEY AWOKE, minutes or maybe hours later, and knew instinctively that she was alone. She shot to a sitting position in the big bed, her hand reaching out for the place where Ben should have been.

He's gone, she thought in sudden panic. *He's left me again!*

But no, his clothes were in a crumpled heap on the velvet-covered chair by the bed. He wouldn't have gone any farther than the front door of her apartment with-

out his clothes, she told herself as sweet reason merci-
fully returned. She lay back on the pillows, sighing
contentedly, to wait for him to return to her from wherever he'd gone. Barely a moment later, she heard a low,
muffled curse and sat up again to see Ben's shape silhou-
etted by the faint light shining in the foyer behind him.

"Ben," she called softly, reaching out to turn on the
silk-shaded lamp by the bed. It cast a warm, pink glow
over his naked body. "Are you okay?"

"Stubbed my toe," he mumbled and then held up an
opened bottle of champagne. "I got thirsty," he said with
a grin. "Here." He handed her two champagne flutes,
leaning over the bed to release the folded sheaf of papers
tucked under his arm. "Hold these while I get in." He
pulled back the covers, the champagne bottle still held
in one hand, and climbed into bed beside her. Fluffing up
the pillows behind him, he leaned back and grinned at
her happily. "Aren't you going to read them?" he asked,
indicating the folded papers in her lap.

"What is it?" she asked hesitantly, almost afraid to
touch them. He'd mentioned some papers he had for her
to sign. These, then, were them.

"Open it," he urged, grinning, as he took the champagne glasses from her.

Stacey shrugged and picked up the legal-size document. Very slowly, she unfolded it and began to read. In
a few minutes she looked up at him, her eyes wide. "But,
Ben," she said as if he didn't already know what it con-
tained, "this is a deed to Iron Oakes. To half of Iron
Oakes," she corrected herself. "In my name! I don't understand. It's yours now. Henry's will—"

Ben plucked the papers from her fingers, replacing
them with a brimming glass of champagne. "After a great
deal of thought, I came to the considered opinion that

Henry wrote that clause with the sole intention of forcing you to stay on at Iron Oakes once you finally came
back," he told her. "He never said anything, but I think
he knew how I feel about you," he said gently. "I think
he always knew. Or maybe Marta told him. And I think
maybe he thought that if he got you to come back and
stay for a while, then I would do the rest and keep you
there for good."

"This is why you came all this way? To give me this?"

He nodded. "I thought if I came in person instead of
mailing it that you might give me another chance."

"But—" Emotion clogged her voice.

He placed a gentle finger over her lips. "It's yours," he
said firmly. "No matter what." He lifted his glass and
clicked it against hers. "To us," he said, leaning over to
kiss her softly before he drank.

"To us," Stacey agreed, staring at him over the rim of
her glass. She couldn't believe it—the ranch and Ben, too,
sitting here in her bed!

Propped up among the frilly white linens, with the
champagne glass in his hand, he looked like some virile
Arabian sheikh at leisure with his favorite concubine.
The lacy comforter pulled up around his lean middle
made his furred chest look harder and broader in contrast. The pink glow all around him from the bedside
lamp and the silk bed hangings made his tanned face and
hard-muscled arms look darker, and his hair blacker.
Everything, in fact, that was masculine about him
seemed more so set against the ultrafeminine surroundings of her bedroom.

"Oh, I do love you, Ben!" she burst out impulsively,
suddenly giddy with happiness and love.

"Enough to marry me?" he asked. "No, wait," he held
up his hand as she started to answer him. "Think about

it, Stacey. Think hard. Do you love me enough to give up all this?" he said, making a motion with his glass that took in the room and her apartment with all its chic elegance and all the sophisticated people who went with that kind of environment. "Enough to come back to Texas with me? Back to that dusty little ranch and its dirty cattle and hick cowboys?" He tossed her words back at her. "This cowboy in particular?"

"Oh, Ben. I didn't mean that!" she cried. "You know I didn't mean any of it! I just said it because I was hurt and angry and so—" she hesitated and then plunged ahead "—so full of wounded pride that I couldn't see straight. I said the worst things I could think of to hurt you, too."

"Well, you did," he said seriously. "You nearly broke my heart clean in two."

"Oh, Ben. I'm sorry. I—"

He put a finger to her lips. "No, don't say it. We've both said and done a passel of things we're sorry for. Let's just forget them and start over from here, okay?"

"But, I—" There was so much she wanted to say. So much to apologize for and explain.

"Okay?" he said again.

Stacey nodded. "Okay." She pursed her lips against his finger in a fleeting kiss. "I love you so much," she whispered, turning her face up to his.

"I love you, too." He kissed her tenderly. "More than I can ever tell you."

She smiled dreamily and tilted her head to nuzzle his throat. Her mouth opened against his skin, tasting the salty-sweetness of him. She felt him shiver under the touch of her lips. "Try to tell me," she said as the fierce flame of love and desire flickered hotly through her veins, making her want him again. She kissed his neck and shoulders and whatever else she could reach while they were both holding champagne glasses. "Show me how much you love me."

Without a word, Ben turned, reaching sideways and slightly behind him to set his champagne glass on the nightstand.

On impulse Stacey tilted her own glass, spilling what was left of the icy contents over her bare breasts. It trickled coldly down her stomach, making her shiver, but Ben didn't seem to notice what she'd done. She giggled under her breath and handed him her glass to put on the nightstand next to his.

"Now," he said, turning back to take her into his arms again. "This time we're going to do it my way. Nice and slow and—Geez!" he yelped as his torso came into contact with her wet breasts and belly. "What's this?"

"My champagne. I spilled it," she explained, laughing softly, "all over me. It's sticky," she complained, glancing up at him from under her lashes, "and cold." She shivered delicately to emphasize her point.

Ben grinned wickedly and pushed her down into the pillows. "Poor baby is cold," he drawled, an expression of mock concern in his blue eyes as he bent his head and began to lick at the sticky wetness on her breasts. "I'll fix it," he said. "I'll make you nice and warm again." He lifted his head for a moment to look into her lambent eyes. His own were burning with love and passion and single-minded determination. "But it's going to take a long, slow time," he warned her. "And you're going to be on fire before I'm finished."

Stacey laughed in pure glee and pulled him down to her again. "Take as long as you want," she whispered. "I like the heat."

COMING NEXT MONTH

#285 STRICTLY BUSINESS
Bobby Hutchinson

Sophie Larson was appalled when Rio Agostini moved his
motorcycle business next door to her exclusive clothing
boutique. But to her surprise, his lusty charm actually drew
women to her store. And once Sophie got the benefit of all
that lustiness herself . . . she discovered that leather and lace
mixed and matched very well indeed.

#286 TOGETHER AGAIN Ruth Jean Dale

When Brodie Farrell appeared on her doorstep, Kate was
horrified. Her recent divorce had been a blow to her ego,
and she'd fortified herself with calories galore. The "little"
Katie Ward Brodie had known from school days was no
more. But pound for luscious pound, there was certainly
more woman to love. . . .

#287 THE PIRATE Jayne Ann Krentz

Historical author Katherine Inskip had given up hope of
finding a man like the men she wrote about—and fantasized
about—in real life. Swashbuckling pirate types just didn't
blend with the bland, modern-day landscape. That's how
Katherine knew Jared Hawthorne was the real thing: he was
almost too macho for even *her* to handle. Almost . . .

#288 FOREVER MINE, VALENTINE
Vicki Lewis Thompson
EDITOR'S CHOICE

Jill Amory, decorator of mall windows, was not shopping
for a husband, but a distinguished gent named Charlie
Hartman had matchmaking high on his list. He insisted that
on Valentine's Day Jill would be looking into the eyes of the
man she would marry. And why did she get the strange
feeling that Charlie had *something* to do with putting
Spencer Jegger so persistently—and irresistibly—in
her path?

A compelling novel of deadly revenge and passion
from Harlequin's bestselling international
romance author Penny Jordan

Eleven years had passed but the
terror of that night was something
Pepper Minesse would never
forget. Fueled by revenge against
the four men who had brutally
shattered her past, she set in
motion a deadly plan to destroy
their futures.

Available in February!

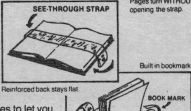

H A R L E Q U I N
American Romance®

**Beginning next month
Share in the**

Rocky Mountain Magic

Join American Romance in celebrating the magical
charm of the Colorado Rockies at a very special place—
The Stanley Hotel. Meet three women friends whose lives
are touched with magic and who will never be the same,
who find love in a very special way, the way of
enchantment.

Read and love
#329 BEST WISHES by Julie Kistler, February 1990
#333 SIGHT UNSEEN by Kathy Clark, March 1990 and
#337 RETURN TO SUMMER by Emma Merritt, April 1990

ROCKY MOUNTAIN MAGIC—All it takes is an open heart.
Only from Harlequin American Romance

All the Rocky Mountain Magic Romances take place at
the beautiful Stanley Hotel.

RMM-1

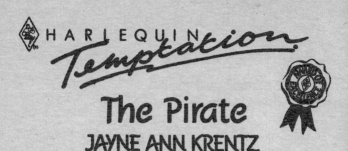

The Pirate
JAYNE ANN KRENTZ

At the heart of every powerful romance story lies a
legend. There are many romantic legends and
countless modern variations on them, but they all
have one thing in common: They are tales of brave,
resourceful women who must gentle and tame the
powerful, passionate men who are their true mates.

The enormous appeal of Jayne Ann Krentz lies in
her ability to create modern-day versions of these
classic romantic myths, and her LADIES AND
LEGENDS trilogy showcases this talent. Believing
that a storyteller who can bring legends to life
deserves special attention, Harlequin has chosen
the first book of the trilogy—THE PIRATE—to
receive our Award of Excellence. Look for it in
February.

AE-PIR-1